Valerie Martin's A RECENT MARTYR

"An irresistible force. For sex, perhaps the nearest equivalent is Anne Rice/Anne Rampling.... For an understanding of an unexpected love's ability to turn one's universe upside down, Iris Murdoch. Martin does it all, and does it very wonderfully indeed."

— *Village Voice*

"Surprising and shocking. A dark, heady...powerful novel."

— *San Francisco Chronicle*

"Martin's exotic, contemporary New Orleans [is] a mesmerizing landscape of decay and rebirth."

— *Kirkus Reviews*

"A memorable novel, redolent with the tropical corruption that is so much a part of the charm of New Orleans. Martin's prose is clean, precise and to the point—gives much pleasure. A subtle, witty novel."

— *Publishers Weekly*

Also by VALERIE MARTIN

Set in Motion
Alexandra
The Consolation of Nature and Other Stories

A Recent Martyr

A
Recent
Martyr

Valerie Martin

VINTAGE CONTEMPORARIES

Vintage Books
A Division of Random House, Inc.
New York

Thanks to Barbara Deming, M.D., for invaluable
information about bubonic plague.

First Vintage Contemporaries Edition, August 1989

Copyright © 1987 by Valerie Martin

All rights reserved under International and Pan-American Copyright
Conventions. Published in the United States by Random House, Inc.,
New York. Originally published, in hardcover, by Houghton Mifflin
Company, Boston, in 1987.

Library of Congress Cataloging-in-Publication Data
Martin, Valerie.
A recent martyr/Valerie Martin.
p.   cm. — (Vintage contemporaries)
Originally published: Boston: Houghton Mifflin, 1987.
ISBN 0-679-72158-4: $7.95
I. Title.
[PS3563.A7295R4   1989]
813'.54—dc19

88-82386
CIP

Manufactured in the United States of America
10 9 8 7 6 5 4 3 2 1

for M . A .

That we are in ourselves hateful, reason alone will convince us; and yet there is no religion but the Christian which teaches us to hate ourselves; wherefore no other religion can be entertained by those who know themselves to be worthy of nothing but hatred.

Blaise Pascal, *Pensées*

A Recent Martyr

ONE

TODAY I took my daughter, Christine, for a ride on the streetcar. We live on the other side of town, near the Industrial Canal, in an area that could be called the back side of the city. Before the epidemic our neighborhood showed some mild symptoms of becoming fashionable, for the houses are old, solid, and inexpensive, as well as convenient to the French Quarter, which is distinctly fashionable. But now, because the death tolls continue to be highest north of Canal Street, people only think of moving away when they can. My own house would sell today for half what I paid for it scarcely five years ago.

To get to the streetcar, we took the Desire bus to Canal Street, then walked the few blocks to St. Charles Avenue, where the streetcar line ends. I held Chris's hand as we stood before the open doors of the car and watched the crowd pouring out. She looked at the people and I looked at her. Her expression was tense; she worried that getting on the car might prove more difficult than she had anticipated. She didn't want me to drag her on behind me, but she wouldn't release my hand for fear of being separated from me. When she saw her chance, she stepped forward and I followed. We accomplished the two steps in unison, without bumping anyone or pulling at each other. As she dropped the coins I had given her into the clanging machine, she cast me an approving look. Sometimes I couldn't please her, I was an embarrassment to her, but at the moment we were a fine, graceful pair and even her critical eye could find nothing to censure. I hid my amusement at the way she surveyed the car and chose her seat. Once she was in it, and I at her side, she relaxed and gave herself over to the intense pleasure of being on the streetcar. She looked about avidly, at the other passengers, at the advertisements, at the driver, and, when the bell rang noisily and the car lurched forward, she touched my knee with her fingertips and whispered, "Here we go."

As we passed through the business section I found myself oddly excited. The quarantine had been lifted months earlier, but still it was a pleasure to move freely about the city. I couldn't help valuing this freedom, as I had so recently done without it. Chris and I had planned this trip carefully. We would ride the car to the park, have our lunch, which I carried in a paper bag, walk among the great oaks, where I would be free to listen to my own thoughts while Chris pursued squirrels and birds, and then return as we had come. When the car rattled around the long curve at Lee Circle, I observed from my window a couple who stood waiting for a bus. The man had his arm about the woman's shoulders. She leaned against him with an air of studied indolence. My mind had already begun to wander and as it did it turned up, with irritating irregularity, as a horse's hooves will turn up stones on a roadbed, startling and vivid memories of Pascal. One flew up before me, complete and irresistible. It came from an early period of our affair, before the quarantine, before the epidemic, before Claire.

He had requested that I not wear any underclothes when we were together, and so, whenever possible, I did as he asked. Sometimes I carried a pair of underpants in my purse but as time went on I grew bold and went about absently, forgetting that there was nothing beneath my skirt. It amused me, seemed harmless enough, and pleased Pascal immensely. He liked to rest his hand on my buttocks when we walked outdoors together and in those moments when we were unobserved, in elevators, in parks, in the dark back rooms of bookstores and bars, he would often slip his hand beneath my skirt, amusing himself, he said, at how wide-eyed such behavior left me.

One morning I was leaving his apartment and he came out with me, drowsy, complaining of the hour which was only just past dawn, to wait with me for the bus. His apartment was in a nonresidential area, downtown near the river, and the scenery was, for the most part, the fronts and sides of warehouses. The street was deserted. I leaned against the wall of his building, for the bus stop was only a step away, and he pressed himself against me, kissing me lazily, working his hands slowly down my back and up again. Now and then I leaned out over his shoulder to see if a bus was coming. At last, far down the street, I saw one. I stepped away from the wall and Pascal came with me, holding me by my waist and turning my back to the street. He began to kiss me seriously and to press my hips against his. I enjoyed this until the bus was a few moments away. I should be taking my fare from my purse, I thought, but Pascal held me so tightly I couldn't move. He had pulled my blouse free from my skirt and pushed it up so that, in another moment, my breasts would be exposed. I laughed and pushed him away. He redoubled his hold on me and put his mouth over mine, muffling my weak protest.

I could hear the bus now, though I couldn't turn my head to see it. Pascal had his tongue halfway down my throat and showed no sign of relenting. I struggled, but to no avail. Now the bus had pulled up to the curb and I heard the doors snap open at my back.

Pascal continued to caress me. He had begun to gather up the back of my skirt in his hands so that I felt the hem rising above my knees. I understood, with a sinking heart, what was about to happen, but the bus driver, who sat at the wheel looking down at us, didn't have a clue.

"I hate to break this up," he said petulantly, "but you want to get on this bus?"

For answer Pascal pulled my skirt up quickly, gathering it in around my waist. I heard the driver's sudden intake of breath, but then for a moment he was silent. Pascal released my mouth at last and I hid my face against his chest. I was, I knew, scarlet with embarrassment, but somehow the thing struck me as so wildly funny that I stifled both laughter and tears. Pascal was resetting my body against his own so that he could get his hand between my legs. He pressed his fingers deep inside, forcing my legs apart so that I had to brace myself against him to keep from falling.

"Man," the bus driver said, "what are you doing?"

Pascal lifted his head and looked at the man. His fingers were so deep inside me that he touched the wall of my womb and I forgot where I was. Then I heard the doors snap closed and the engine rev up. A blast of the exhaust warmed my legs as the exasperated driver left us behind.

Pascal lifted me then and carried me back into his apartment.

"Suppose he calls the police?" I said.

He smiled. He was heading determinedly for his bed-room.

"I don't think he will," he said.

"What did he look like?"

He threw me down across the bed and climbed in after me. "He was big and fat and black," he said, "and his eyes were about to fall out of his head."

"Suppose he'd gotten out of the bus?"

"We would have had to run for it."

I laughed. "I thought I would die," I said.

"You have a lovely ass," Pascal observed, turning me over. "It made his day."

Then, because I could hear Pascal removing his jeans, and because I knew there wouldn't be another bus for fifteen minutes, I began pulling pillows in under my stomach and arranging myself to receive him. I was sad and excited and so completely humiliated that I found myself hoping that he would hurt me. Abruptly he grabbed me by the groin and pulled me back toward him. I let myself be pushed about, put into place, my arms out before me, my cheek against the cool sheet, my knees braced beneath me. "Do it hard," I said hopelessly.

"As hard as I can?" he asked.

"Yes," I said. "I'm not afraid."

This memory passed behind my eyes intact as I sat on the streetcar. I looked about nervously, as if someone else might have seen it. But the faces around me were all lost in their own reveries. Some looked serenely out at the large houses, the wide tree-shaded street; others ignored even the scenery, so deep had they fallen into their own imaginings. No one so much as returned my look. Each pondered, as I did, the other, the secret self.

TWO

THE FIRST time Pascal saw Claire, though he looked directly at her, he didn't know he had seen her. He was thinking of three things at once and in none of these thoughts did her image figure, so that although his eyes rested on her profile, which was discreetly and, he was to learn, characteristically lowered, he made no note of it. He was listening to the music that was pouring into the dome-shaped air of the church and thinking that he had not expected anything written by Mendelssohn to be so agreeable. Another train of thought, so often pursued that it was more a recollection than an idea, concerned his deep abhorrence of the Roman Catholic Church as it is today (or as he believed it to be), controlled and populated by hysterical women, homosexuals, lesbians, and sanctimonious bastards like his father.

Pascal's father was a devout Catholic, a man who went on periodic retreats, cultivated the company of priests, and had disowned one of his sons for refusing to bring up his children in the true faith. He kept one missal on his nightstand and another at his office, both crammed with holy pictures. He taught his children, at a tender age, to kiss these pictures, an activity they could not undertake often enough to please him. He hated Negroes, Italians, and

Cubans, and could become so enraged at any insinuation that Christ didn't share his prejudices that he would strike whoever disputed this conviction. He was a small, thin man who could have been knocked unconscious by a well-placed blow from any of his grown sons, but, for their mother's sake, they had never raised a hand against him.

Pascal, an intelligent, nearsighted, introverted child, had despised his father from birth. He couldn't remember a pleasant conversation, a span of ten minutes, in which his father had failed to arouse his complete contempt. But more than he hated his father, he hated the Church, for it was the Church, he had early perceived, that allowed his father to scale the peaks of hypocrisy, untouched by reason or fact, the confirmation of his own righteousness ever set before him by the adulation of priests.

The other perversion the Church tolerated, which Pascal could not, was the role his mother was forced to play. She was, unlike his father, truly devout and she was more distressed by her own failings than those of others. She expected to carry a cross, was willing to do so, and her husband was the burden she chose to bear, uncomplaining and steadfast, to the grave and beyond it. That Pascal could not get her to share his unflattering opinion of his father's true nature was what he could not bear, for he loved his mother with a child's pure passion and wanted her freedom as dearly as he wanted his own. And it was the Church, he observed, that enslaved her, even more than her husband, and with the aid of her husband. When Pascal was young, his father and the Church became confused in his mind, nor did he make an effort to put an end to this confusion as he grew older. Rage suited him, so he kept it.

As he sat in the Cathedral, listening to Mendelssohn's

oratorio, he thought of the corrupt Church and he reflected that he had, apart from some superior verses by Hopkins, no reason to believe it had ever been different. His eyes rested upon Claire and he noted the modest direction of her gaze. He thought, case in point. He looked at the program in his lap, unconscious of the fact (nor did he ever know it) that he had imitated her and was to imitate her again. He meant only to read the title of Mendelssohn's piece, for he thought it was certainly worth listening to.

Claire wouldn't have agreed, though she was not un-affected by the music. She was in the state of mind that often afflicted her when listening to concerts of religious music, which she did as often as possible. She had been drawn into the music and then, mysteriously, lifted by it, buoyed up by it, until she lost all touch with it and could not have described, or even recognized again, what she heard. She listened instead, and not without wonder, to the insistent pulsing of her own heart.

THREE

THE SECOND time Pascal saw Claire she kindled in him, against his will, the sentiment that he was to experience again and again, and always against his will: the most grudging respect. She had come to dinner at his father's house at the invitation of the priest who was the real, the expected guest.

"Father James is bringing a young woman with him," Pascal's father said as he hung up the phone. His face betrayed neither suspicion nor interest in this announcement, but was molded into the pious mask he slipped over his features whenever he spoke of or to Father James.

Pascal, who was lying on the couch drinking a beer in lazy conversation with his brother Jean, raised his eyebrows and laughed.

"I don't see that there's anything funny in that, Pascal," his father remarked.

Pascal addressed his brother. "You'd think these priests would leave their conquests at church, where they belong."

"That's a stupid remark," his father pointed out. "This young woman is very devout. I've met her before; most discreet and truly pious. I wish you would take an interest in such a person."

Pascal smiled benignly at his father. "I prefer whores," he said.

"And besides," his father added, turning away, "Father James is her confessor and old enough to be her father."

Pascal sat for some time after this conversation, wondering whether it would be better to stay home and bait this priest and his prodigy or go downtown and get drunk. His brother got to his feet and declared his intention to seduce the young woman, no matter how ugly she was, and to save some item of her clothing to show his father when he had been successful. Pascal decided to stay for this show.

An hour later the priest's black Chevrolet turned into the long driveway that led to the Toussaints' house and Father James got out on the driver's side. The sight of this automobile enraged Pascal, for at that time few people had access to gasoline. The city exercised discretion, buses continued to run right to the end, but the Church was to spend its supply, much to the chagrin of the priest, who dusted off his black pants in the driveway, in a matter of weeks. Pascal, standing at the kitchen window, could see Claire clearly. He was surprised by what he saw and yelled to his brother, "It could be worse. Much worse." Father James crossed in front of the car and opened the door. Claire turned sideways in her seat and, before she stood up, looked through the window at Pascal. Her lips were pressed together in a thin, impatient line, and she appeared to be annoyed at something Father James was saying. He held out his hand to her and she looked at it indifferently, then stepped out without touching him. Father James was talking, nor did he stop talking as he followed her across the driveway, across the lawn, out of Pascal's field of vision, to the front door.

Pascal felt a momentary confusion. The young woman he had seen was not what he had expected. She looked neither humble nor penitent, nor simply mindless. She had not met his gaze, though he felt certain that she had seen him there and averted her eyes out of annoyance rather than humility. He had been impressed by the way her long blond hair framed her face, sweeping over the tops of her ears to the heavy braid that lay across her shoulder like a straying golden snake. Her eyes and skin were very light, her clothes dark and plain. He had noted, in that brief look, a thin edge of white lace visible at the neck of her blouse. It was a gray silk blouse, with the top button undone, the bodice gathered in tiny flat pleats, a fashion, Pascal thought as he turned from the window, he had always liked. He went into the living room, where his father had already claimed the priest's attention. Claire stood in the doorway, looking coldly at the back of the priest's balding head. Pascal noted the small black cross at her neck and smirked to himself. She was a real bitch, he thought. Jean would have a fine time of it.

Then the priest turned to her and introduced her all around. She held her hand out and repeated the name of each person as it was given to her. When Pascal's turn came he took her hand forcefully and looked her full in the face. The hand was cold and the eyes he looked into went suddenly out of focus in a way that made him want to grasp her chin and shake her. She said his name and eased her hand out of his grip, then turned to his mother. There were a few uncomfortable moments of conversation. Father James explained that Claire was doing such fine work with the catechism classes, she would soon be running the whole program alone. She was so competent and worked such long hours, set such an example for the children and the adults in the congregation, they were certainly fortunate to have her back.

She had been away, it turned out, in a convent school in Lacombe for ten years and now she had been turned loose upon the secular world. Pascal watched her as her virtues were tallied up before her. She didn't seem to be listening. Her eyes wandered over the objects in the room. They settled on a crucifix that hung above the door between the living room and the dining room. Her mouth opened slightly as she looked at it, and then her tongue came out and moistened first the upper then the lower lip. She dropped her eyes from the figure on the cross and looked for the first time directly at Pascal. He smiled and she, shyly, looking away even as she did it, smiled back.

He felt a rush of interest. It started somewhere in his legs and rushed up over him, a familiar and beloved sensation, the results of which had, in the past, included pleasure as well as pain. He determined to talk to her before she left, perhaps to touch her if he could. The group began to move toward the dining room, where the table was waiting, already laden with food. Pascal followed behind his father and Jean. Ten years in a convent, he thought. What a criminal thing to do to a decent-looking woman.

His mother directed them to their chairs. Pascal's was across from Claire; Jean was next to her. The brothers exchanged a look that Pascal was unable to interpret, though he suspected that Jean, for some reason, had decided against his plan. Father James and Pascal's father were deep in a conversation about the physical improvements at the retreat house in Abbeville. The new chapel had twice as much room and the additional dining hall allowed for larger groups on one-day retreats. Pascal's mother, who had never been there but knew the area, recalled walking along the little river that ran behind the seminary. "We used to look up at the dark windows and wave if we saw anyone," she said. "We thought it was a prison."

Father James laughed. He had spent four years in that seminary, and the comparison was not without its ironic aspects, he assured her. Pascal, serving mashed potatoes to himself, observed that iron bars do not a prison make. His father frowned. The subject changed to a recent retreat his father had taken at the house in question.

"I try to go for a few days at least twice a year," he said to Claire, who was gazing into a bowl of green beans as she piled them into her plate. Pascal noticed that she passed the roast beef without taking any, a sure sign, he thought, of culinary fastidiousness. She was probably a vegetarian, which accounted for the translucence of her skin. "It refreshes me," his father went on. "When I come back I feel ready to take up my work again."

Father James expounded on the benefit of such periods of recollection, explaining how serious was the need for them in a world where little was held sacred. Claire, chewing her beans, looked at him coldly. It gave Pascal a pleasant thrill to see her glare in this way at his lifelong enemy.

"Claire looks," he observed, "as if she doesn't agree."

She put her fork down in her plate and looked at it, blushing deeply. Pascal's father gave him a considered scowl. How he wished his children shared with him some of the joys of religion. But they preferred, he explained, to have contempt for him and to assume that everyone else did too. This was one of the many burdens he had to carry, one of the things he pondered on his retreats: how he could have fathered Godless children. As he made this last remark, he looked at his wife with an expression that placed the blame for the phenomenon squarely upon her head. What a pleasure it must be to Claire's parents, he added, to have raised a good Catholic girl.

Claire had not looked up. "Still," Pascal insisted, "I think Claire didn't agree with you."

Father James turned to Claire. "Isn't that for her to say?" he suggested.

Claire looked up at last, and an interesting silence settled upon the group. "I don't see," she said after a moment, "why Christ should have suffered the agony of His crucifixion so that Christians might sit about in air-conditioned comfort feeling good about it."

Pascal choked on his wine. His father, dumfounded, looked from his son to Father James to his wife, avoiding at all costs Claire's composed features.

Father James sighed. "Perhaps you've been out of the world too long to be tolerant of it," he said.

Claire raised her eyebrows in disbelief. She looked at the priest and for a moment Pascal thought she would respond. But something she saw there made her lower her eyes, and she said submissively, "That's true."

The subject was closed. Pascal watched her carefully for the rest of the meal but never met her eyes. She didn't eat another bite of her food and when they rose to go to the living room for coffee, she folded her napkin and placed it beside her nearly full plate. Pascal followed close behind her. Father James and Pascal's father settled themselves on the couch, used to one another's company and deep in a volley of mutual adulation. Jean, giving Pascal a shrug, declined to join them and excused himself, saying that he had to meet his wife and son at his in-laws' house. Pascal's mother disappeared into the kitchen, leaving Pascal and Claire standing uneasily in the doorway. There was another small couch and two chairs, turned on either side of a marble-topped end table so that whoever sat in them would be slightly withdrawn from the rest of the company and directed toward each other. Pascal made for one of these chairs, and Claire, after a moment, went to the other. She sat down on the edge of it and folded her hands in her lap, looking so uncomfortable that Pascal pitied her.

"I thought what you said was great," he said.

She gave him a weary look. "I shouldn't have said it. I don't know why I did."

"But you were right."

"No. Father James was right. Christ's love is something to rejoice over and it's true that a recollected soul can find great comfort, as it should, in this love."

Pascal gave her an incredulous look. "What bullshit," he said.

Claire looked away and said nothing.

"You know that's ridiculous, that crap about Christ's love. If Christ loves a hypocrite like my father, He is lacking in any powers of discrimination."

"The question is not whether He can love your father. Can He love you?"

"I don't give a damn about that."

"I can see that," she said. "I saw that when I came in."

"And what do you make of it?"

"There's nothing to be made of it, as far as I can tell."

"Surely I should be made to see the error of my ways."

"I don't think you are likely to be dissuaded from your errors by talking to me."

"What touching humility," Pascal said.

(15)

"No," Claire replied, leaning forward in her chair, "it isn't humility. It's that I don't think anyone could be dissuaded from error by talking to anyone. It doesn't have anything to do with talk."

"Then with what?" Pascal smiled to himself. Now, he thought, she would doubtless give him some wild-eyed description of grace.

"What amuses you?" she asked.

"This posture of yours. Did you learn it at school? It doesn't suit you."

She met his eyes at last, but only for a moment. She looked then at Father James and Mr. Toussaint. Father James was describing a deathbed visit he had made the night before. Mr. D., a notorious unbeliever, whose wife had been praying for him day and night for twenty-five years, died screaming for a priest. "I could hear him when I opened the car door," Father James said. "All the way out in the street." The dying man calmed down as soon as he saw the canonical collar. He prepared and made a full confession, and received the last rites only moments before his final breath. His wife sat weeping throughout, thinking, no doubt, of the years she had spent on her knees so that this moment might arrive. "She followed me down stairs, weeping and making prayers of thanksgiving," Father James concluded.

Pascal was looking at Claire as she listened to this description. Abruptly she smiled broadly, but not, Pascal thought, from pleasure. Then she frowned and looked away.

"It's bunk," Pascal said. "And you know it."

"I should never have left the convent," she said.

"You're lucky you got out alive."

"I'll be all right," she replied, though she didn't look at Pascal, "if I can find a confessor."

"I'm sure you have a great deal to confess," Pascal observed. "I'll bet Father James is just stunned by the depravity of your imagination."

She looked up quickly. "I wish he were," she said. "Unfortunately he thinks my desire to be better than I am is my greatest fault."

"So you're damned if you do and damned if you don't."

Claire laughed. It was the first time Pascal had seen her laugh and it took him by surprise. He had not thought her capable of genuine amusement, but she was delighted by his remark and looked on him with sudden affection. "That is," she said, "often the position of the soul in its converse with God."

"Why spend so much time thinking about God?" he replied impatiently. "There's plenty to worry about without worrying about God."

"What I can never understand," she said, "is how anyone can think of anything else."

Pascal gave her a cold look.

"I don't think of God because I want to," she continued. "I think of Him because I think of Him. I don't feel this possibility others seem to feel, of doing without these thoughts."

"You've been brainwashed," Pascal replied.

"It's you who have been brainwashed," she said tartly, "if you seriously imagine that there's anything more important in your own life than the ultimate fate of your own soul."

Pascal frowned. Father James was stirring sugar into his coffee, smiling at Claire and Pascal over his cup with such false gaiety that Pascal, who glanced his way, experienced a deepening consternation. "Be careful, Pascal," Father James warned him. "She might convert you."

"And then where would you be?" his father chimed in.

"I would be as big a hypocrite as you are," Pascal snapped. He turned to Claire to see her reaction to this gallantry and found her studying the arm of her chair.

A silence fell on the group and it was heavy with the disapproval of the two older men. Pascal sat smiling at Claire's profile until his mother, mercifully entering with a tray of sweets and too eagerly assisted by her husband, began a conversation about gardening. Father James, who grew the most breathtaking roses in the parish, gave her unsolicited advice. Banana peels laid just below the surface of the soil were well known to increase the size and fragrance of the bloom. Beneath the priest's raised voice, Pascal was able to address Claire without being overheard. "What are you thinking?" he asked.

She started, looking up at him blankly. "Thinking?" she said.

"You were annoyed with me for what I said."

"Not annoyed," she said. "I did wonder why you bother."

"It's never a bother to me to suggest to my father the real destination of his devotional trek."

"But why should that make any difference to you? Why should you be concerned with another person's progress when you've no concern for your own?"

"Yet I feel certain that you've judged my progress on the basis of ten minutes of talk."

"The only judgment I've made about you is that you seem very determined to trip me up."

Pascal laughed. "That's accurate. And my resolution is firm."

"What is it you hope to make me say?" she asked.

"I don't care what you say. It's what I hope to make you do that interests me."

Claire sat up straight, drawing her feet in under the chair. Her mouth opened slightly, then closed again, and she blushed. Pascal smiled, stretching his legs out before him, thoroughly pleased with himself. She was, he thought, lovely, innocent. Would she be worth the effort? His eyes fell on her wrist, thin and pale at the edge of her sleeve, turned up toward him, and he saw the blue vein raised beneath the white flesh. He had a momentary desire to press his mouth to that vein. To quiet himself he averted his eyes, then raised them to Claire's face, surprised to find her looking directly at him. Her expression puzzled him, for it was a mixture of interest and contempt, as if she saw in him something she had been expecting to see. Abruptly she turned her gaze to Father James, who was discoursing on different methods of pruning Grandiflora roses. She waited until he paused and then suggested that, since they had both to be back at the church shortly, they should think of leaving. Her manner was so proprietary that the priest gave in at once, and Pascal could not help being amused. He made one or two attempts to get her attention again but was unsuccessful, and in a few minutes she and her protector had said their goodbyes and gone out across the lawn. Pascal stood on the porch, watching to see if she would look back, but she didn't. He went inside and threw himself down on the couch. He was annoyed.

FOUR

—

AT the time Pascal met Claire and spoke to me about her, I had reached in my own life such a low ebb I sometimes felt, listening to him, that I couldn't lift my head to respond. When he wasn't with me, however, things were worse, and so I said nothing or even encouraged him with a question or two. I had always known the worst about Pascal, that he was faithless, that he liked himself that way; and though I loved him, I had too much sense to expect much in return. It was enough that he came to see me whenever he could and didn't pry into the state of my marriage.

My marriage was nearly over and I knew it. All my efforts to explain this failure to myself led me to one conclusion: I had always intended it to fail. And to another, more painful: that I could never have loved my husband much if I could feel as I did now. What I felt in his presence was the most perfect numbness; it was as if my senses shut down when he came into the room. It was painful for him, but more painful for me, wanting, as I did, things to be different. I felt I had changed, become hard, brittle, and it was as if I looked out through something thin, hard, like glass. I saw for myself a future of unrewarding jobs, days that stretched out meaninglessly. I had no wish to destroy myself nor to endure, so what was there, I thought, to do? This consciousness of a lack of intention, of my own unwillingness to make decisions, save those which would lead to a more realized exile from those people who loved me, made me sad company. I knew, of course, that my situation was not unusual.

Pascal was, in fact, in the same condition, but with less to fall back on than I had. What interested me about him was the tenacity with which he held to certain views that were contrary to his own interest. Formed by nature to be an extraordinary man, with physical strength and a thoroughgoing intelligence, he suffered the misfortune of knowing himself to be so and of not knowing what good it might do him. He was not the first man I had met who could not accept, because of his intelligence, the benefits that intelligence might be most likely to provide. He could not think of his own soul without noticing that the people he knew who were concerned with their own souls were uniformly and obviously hypocritical. His love of good literature was impaired by his distaste for the people who taught it, and for the mindless way in which this instruction was received by his fellow students. In short, he found it difficult to be satisfied long in the company of others, for he found no virtue in anything, nor did he want to find it. And yet his nature was generous and he experienced from time to time uncontrollable elations, which were generally caused by the initiation of a love affair, resulting in such a sense of well-being that he might have described himself as tolerably happy.

When I thought of him in this way, which I did too often, my own conscience weighed heavily upon me. I loved

Pascal and was vulnerable to him to such a great degree that he could change my mood with a word. I didn't know why I was in love with him or when it had happened to me or why I had fallen so hard, with such swiftness, the way a boulder, dislodged, can do nothing but fall. I had not expected it to happen, even after I knew we would be lovers. (Though I knew *that* the moment I laid eyes on Pascal. How is it that we can see the results of a meeting at once, with not a glimmer of how it will come about, a prophetic knowledge right down to the shoes, without possibility of alteration, without power to doubt or divest it, without, sometimes, even much interest in the fact of its existence?)

Pascal inspired in me the most complex emotions I'd ever experienced. I pitied him and envied him in one breath. When he kissed me I felt myself moving through my emotional range, as if I could draw the certainty I wanted (the certainty of my own response) from his mouth. He confused me in the way he moved, with unexpected grace amidst a general awkwardness, in his conversation, so intense and yet so severely impersonal, and in his face, unpleasant features combined with marvelous symmetry; I didn't know what to make of him.

Though I knew what he wanted to make of me and that from the start. We met in a library, nor did I imagine for a moment I was the first woman he had exchanged that interested look with across the table. It struck me as absurd, like something from television. I felt the intensity of his gaze, and when I had looked up from my book quickly and looked down again, losing my place entirely, I smiled to myself, thinking of scenes in which we would walk along on either side of the long bookcases, peering at each other through the few open spaces.

I was on my lunch break, an hour's respite from my job as the right hand to a fool. That morning, I remember, I had typed a fifteen-page union contract which would allow my employer to wire a new hotel downtown in such a way that it would probably burn down in six months. I made it my business never to stay for more than a few moments in any building he had contracted. The library, fortunately, had been built by out-of-state architects. It was quiet, cool, and five blocks from my office, and it was my habit to rush to its safety as often as possible and indulge myself in the purest escape I could find. That day my escape was *The Monk*, which I was halfway through. Pascal had been trying for a few moments to read the title, printed at the top of each page. He looked at the page, then up at me, smiling to himself and doubtless feeling that thrill of anticipation which I would not always inspire in him, coupled with a certain sense of doom, which he was a master at shaking off, but which showed, sadly enough, in his face whenever he was contemplating a woman he hadn't met but intended to know.

I looked up again and met his eyes. Then, without looking away, I turned my book around so that he could read the title. He glanced at it, then back at me. "That's trash," he said, "but amusing."

"I know it," I replied. I returned my attention to my book. I had determined the nature of his reading matter much earlier, when he came to the table. It was a Penguin edition of seventeenth-century French poetry.

I would think, looking back on it, that we might have had enough sense to avoid each other simply because of the disparity in our reading tastes.

The hour wore on. Beneath my eyes the monk himself was in bed with a woman. Pascal perused his poems, looking up at me occasionally. For a short time I tried to make my face expressionless, then tried to fill it with expression, uncertain how much of my effort was visible to Pascal's close scrutiny. I looked at my watch, allowed seven pages to pass me, and looked again. Then I closed my book and stood up. Pascal put his book down before him and pointed to the window at the end of the bookshelf. "You're not going out in that?" he inquired.

I followed his finger and found myself looking at a plantain tree bent nearly in half by the force of the rain. I forgot Pascal and thought only of the dismal walk I would have back to my office, of the impossibility of calling in to say the rain was keeping me (for in New Orleans rain stops no native), and of my shoes, which were suede and would doubtless be thoroughly ruined. My heart and my shoulders fell. Pascal had gotten up and stood at my side. "How far do you have to go?" he asked.

"A few blocks."

"I've an umbrella," he said, holding this object out before him. "And that gray Volkswagen you can see from here is mine too."

I smiled. At that time people used automobiles sparingly. They rarely appeared downtown.

"And," he added, "it has gasoline in it."

"Really," I said. "How did you manage that."

"My father works for the city," he said.

I paused. The option of getting into a car with a stranger was so rare as to be slightly intimidating.

"Anyway," he said, "it's there, it runs, and I would be happy to take you wherever it is you have to go."

I looked at Pascal, poised for my response, and I felt suddenly weary. "Yes," I said. "I'd appreciate it."

As we walked toward the car, compressing ourselves beneath the umbrella, he took my arm firmly and steered me around puddles as if I were blind. I reflected that it was not an unpleasant feeling, that I truly wished someone would show me where to go, what to do, tell me what to say. He opened the car door, guiding me around him and into the seat, his hand moving from my arm to the small of my back, to my shoulder. Then he closed the door and for a moment I was alone in the damp car. It smelled old and safe and it was quite warm.

The door opened and Pascal joined me, throwing himself onto the seat, closing his umbrella, slamming the door, making, I thought, a great deal of fuss over a fairly simple action. He looked at me twice as he rearranged himself on the seat and fought with his umbrella to get it down on the floor behind him. "May I ask your name?" he said as he turned the key in the ignition.

"Emma," I said.

He smiled. "I'm Pascal. Where are we going, Emma?"

"To Saint Charles and Perdido," I said. "The Planchot Electrical Contractors."

"So you're in wiring."

"No," I said. "I'm in typing."

"That sounds dull."

"Not as dull as it is."

"And you make up for it by spending your lunch hour in the library."

"It's convenient," I said.

"Suppose it were convenient to have lunch with me."

"It could be, if it weren't dull."

He smiled again, but not at me. "You won't know that until afterward."

"I know," I said. I looked out the window at the pouring rain. A man was running along the sidewalk holding a newspaper over his head. I was filled with dismal premonitions. It was seven years since I had made love to anyone but my husband, and my heart ached with fear at the possibility of breaking this long, important fidelity. Would it show on my face? Pascal was suggesting a restaurant, a time, a meeting place, all with such ease and solicitude about my convenience that I thought, Very well, let him manage it all, and if he's good at managing it, then I'll go along.

He pulled the car off the empty street and into a space just steps from the door of my employment. I hesitated. It would be hard to run gracefully into the downpour that awaited me. Pascal began rummaging in the back seat for his umbrella. "It's not necessary," I said. "It's only a few steps."

"None of this is necessary," he said. "That's why we're enjoying it so much." He grasped the umbrella and brought it up, opening his door and leaping out before I could say anything. I watched his face as he crossed in front of the car. He was not looking at me but at one of the spokes on the umbrella, which was broken. He pushed at it with his free hand. His eyes were too close together, his nose too large, and the expression of his mouth the most grimly resolute I had ever seen. He was not, I thought, enjoying any of it very much at all. He just didn't know what else to do. He opened the car door, smiling now and reaching for my arm to help me out. As I put one foot on the pavement, something rushed against it. Pascal stepped back quickly, giving me a look of horrified surprise. It was a rat, as large as a small dog, and it shot out from beneath the car, past Pascal, and away across the pavement with such speed that we both failed to make a sound until it was out of sight.

"Did you see that?" Pascal exclaimed, though there could be no doubt of my answer. I leaned forward on the seat and looked at the curb. We were parked against a storm drain; the rat had come up from the sewer. Pascal had dropped the umbrella and hurried now to retrieve it, though by the time he did so and held it aloft again, shielding my side of the car, we were both completely soaked. Still we went through the motions as if it were important that no more drops touch us. At the door we repeated our agreement for the following day; then I went inside. Alone at my desk I took my shoes off and rubbed the spot where the rat's fur had touched my leg. Never, I thought, had I felt such revulsion at the touch of another living creature.

FIVE

I KNEW very soon that a good deal of the interest I felt for Pascal was the direct result of the way he made me feel about myself. In his company I was strong, devious, devoid of any moral sense, haughty, beautiful, and indolent. I was also a great mystery, even to myself. I walked down the long, red-carpeted hall that ended in our first hotel room as if it were my habit to do so. Pascal walked behind me, his breathing the only sound save the muffled rapping of our footsteps along the hall. When I stopped before the proper door, he reached around me, key in hand, and in a smooth gesture unlocked and opened the door. I stepped inside, turning nervously to face him.

Later I was to see that door closing again and again, in my dreams, in my waking reveries, the door beyond which I was to discover the sweet and unexpected horror of my own nature. I never experienced the shyness I felt, even with my own husband, when I was with Pascal. I was too busy, too absorbed, from the first time. He had a tendency to catch my arms in such a way as to render them useless to me. I can recall vividly still the moment when he rose over me, holding both my arms out at my sides, his strong thumbs pressing insistently into the biceps, pressing and pulling until I thought my arms must come free of the sockets. I was in such a state of excitement that I willingly bore the pain; I don't think I was even conscious of it. "Am I hurting you?" he asked softly, through my helpless moaning. Then I met his eyes, in which I found a peculiar, disinterested variety of sympathy.

"What?" I said. I focused with difficulty on the sense of his question. "No. Not at all."

He smiled, pressing harder. From the waist up we gazed at one another, friendly strangers, though below that our bodies were seriously intertwined. As I became more and more absorbed in the sensations I received from these nether regions, I closed my eyes and turned my face away. An orgasm was hard upon me and I didn't wish to miss its full duration by exchanging remarks or even looks. Then, at the moment of my greatest helplessness, my arms were released. And in that same moment I felt his right hand close about my throat. Still I refused to open my eyes; I was stubborn in my refusal to be distracted. My throat compressed, made a gasping sound; the windpipe was obstructed by Pascal's thumb. At this sound he released me, pulling slowly away from me. But my legs were tight around his hips and I had no intention of giving up what I held so deeply between them.

I opened my eyes. He smiled down at me, but not so surely as before. I put my hands on his shoulders, pulling him down toward me, but instead I found my back abruptly lifted from the sheets. "Now?" he inquired anxiously.

"Yes, please," I said. I sounded, I thought, as if I were responding to an offer of a second helping of potatoes, but Pascal didn't notice. He pulled me in close, one hand against my lower back, the other gripping my shoulder, and then

I felt a series of long shudders pass down his spine, beneath my fingertips. His breathing was rapid, he hid his face against my shoulder, and, after the last spasm had passed, he sucked in air through clenched teeth.

That, as nearly as I can remember, is what happened the first time. I noticed two important things about my lover: he could tell when I had an orgasm, and he could control the moment of his own. These two qualities were rare, I thought, and boded well for our future. I had another thought as I considered his ability to hold back his own orgasm, and that very dangerous thought was this: wouldn't he derive more pleasure if he were forced to lose that control?

A month after that first meeting in the library, I did what I had been talking of doing for years. I told my boss I would work only in the mornings or not at all. To my surprise, he kept me on. After that Pascal and I met regularly. I walked away from these meetings with my blood racing through me, my head awash with new ideas and recollections of our lovemaking, feeling that I had more strength than I could ever spend, even with such a lover as Pascal. By the time I was home, however, this energy was gone and I slid gratefully into a tub of hot water and watched, with a blend of pleasure and horror, the convulsive trembling of my limbs.

Pascal and I were, I sometimes thought, furiously mated. I always excused myself of my passion for him by recalling that I had never intended to have it. I was a lonely wife, a harried mother, a bored employee, and I needed a change, a little desire, an escapade. At first Pascal simply introduced some pleasant possibilities into my cliché-ridden routine, and for this I was grateful. I could, on almost any given day, do everything that was required of me and spend an hour in bed with Pascal as well. The day became the front and the back of that hour, a situation that made everything simultaneously more and less pleasant.

I found, for example, that my temper was short two hours before our meetings, whereas two hours after I could not have been ruffled by an explosion. My daughter avoided me in the mornings and toyed with me in the afternoons, so sensitive was she to my moods. My husband, unfortunately for him, had never been able to apprehend my moods and showed no sign of ever being able to, in spite of his unflagging desire to do so.

It was six months after I met Pascal that I saw Claire for the first time.

SIX

ONE evening, when my husband was away for a few hours and Chris was asleep in her grandmother's house, I met Pascal at a bar on Decatur. We hadn't enough time, we agreed, to take a room and so we sat and talked, drinking furtively and quickly, with an unspoken agreement to get drunk together and see how that was.

For my part I was soon dizzy, sleepy, and disappointed with everything, but particularly with Pascal, who was talking loudly so that the three attractive women at the next table could hear about how, when he was younger and might have taken advantage of it, women rarely went out in the intimate little groups one saw them in now.

I thought of the trouble I had taken to arrange this meeting, of the necessity of my being home in exactly one and a half hours, a good half hour before my husband's earliest possible return. I thought of how I had dressed earlier, what care I had taken in my choice of earrings, shoes, undergarments, in the arrangement of my hair, which I had pinned up and let down three times before leaving it as I always wore it. I remembered calling Chris at my mother's just before I left. "Go to bed on time, darling, when Nana tells you. I'll be there after breakfast in the morning," and of her breathless distracted replies, "Yes, Mommy, I will, Mommy. Will you eat with us? Will we have pancakes?" I should have stayed home with her, I thought, as Pascal smiled at one of the young women and made some comment about the unusual color of her hair. I finished my drink glumly and when Pascal returned his attention to me, offering me another, I declined, saying it was time I left.

Then he was all interest, but it was too late. When we rose to leave I became dizzier still, and though I had no wish to, I was forced to take his arm. He pulled me in close to him, affectionately, sensing my condition but not my reluctance to have his assistance. He steered me through the crowded bar and out into the street.

"Let's walk a bit," I said and he agreed. I pulled away from him as best I could but he didn't release me. He kissed my hair and my neck. "Are you annoyed about something?" he asked.

"No, nothing," I said. "I just drank too much." We walked down Decatur toward the Square. It was just ten o'clock when we reached it; the Cathedral clock rang its jangling bells, *ding-ding, ding-ding*, like ship's bells or the bells at communion when the host is elevated. We walked down the alley alongside the church, past the rectory garden. I had a pebble in my shoe and stopped to remove it, leaning against the iron fence, my foot on the dry stone gutter. Pascal sat down beside me and began to sing softly, making grand faces as if he were singing loudly, an operatic air. I smiled at him and put my hand on his shoulder. He took my hand and kissed it, then pulled me down into a long mindless kiss, our tongues engaged in competitive assaults.

Then there was a noise and we were both apart and on our feet, facing the iron fence. The noise had come from behind it. The rectory door was open and a woman stood in the frame. There were two trees and a good deal of foliage between us, so we saw her unobserved. She came out and threw herself down on a stone bench near the door, not thirty feet from where we stood. Pascal froze at my side and, as I watched him, his expression showed more incredulity than the situation warranted.

"Claire?" he said. The air around us was still, the night so dark and damp that his question seemed to linger on it. The woman jumped to her feet and strode toward us. She had to push her way between an overgrown azalea and the fence, which she did without pause.

"Who is it?" she demanded, coming upon us. She recognized Pascal at once but her face betrayed neither interest nor pleasure. "Pascal," she said. "You frightened me."

Pascal was delighted. "You didn't look frightened. Do you usually run directly at things that frighten you?"

She said nothing; she was looking at me. "This is my friend Emma," Pascal said. "Emma, this is Claire."

I said hello weakly. My clothes were disarranged, my condition, I thought, must be obvious. She was dressed in white, her hair smoothed back, her cheeks a little flushed from the excitement; perfectly neat, perfectly serious.

"What are you doing here?" Pascal indicated the garden.

"I was working for Father Paine. I'm through now."

"Father Paine!" Pascal fairly shouted his amusement at this name.

Claire didn't seem to hear him. She was looking at me again.

"You've given up on Father James then?" Pascal was desperate for her attention.

She didn't look away from me. "What?" she said. "Yes, I'm working here now."

"A true daughter of the Church." Pascal made this observation by way of me. I was embarrassed and stood literally wringing my hands, avoiding Claire's cool and unswerving gaze. Then, giving it up, I raised my eyes to hers.

She smiled at me, a warm, sweet, sympathetic smile I couldn't mistake, and I tried, as best I could, to return it. Then she turned to Pascal. "I have to go now," she said.

"Come out with us." Pascal raised his voice, hoping to stop her, but she had turned away and was walking back the way she had come.

"Good night," she called back softly, and she was gone.

Pascal stood clutching the iron bars of the fence like an imprisoned man. I sat down again on the gutter beside him. I was thoroughly disgusted with him and considered the evening to have been misspent. When his hand strayed to my hair, touching my cheek, I turned my face away. "I have to go home now," I said.

"Is something wrong?"

For a moment I considered saying nothing. I didn't wish to argue with him. But I had drunk too much and my tongue was quick. "I think you asked her to come with us because you knew I would be leaving soon."

He sighed and drew his hand away. "I knew that was it." he said.

"Well?" I stood up and faced him. I wanted to be in my bed, asleep.

"I asked her to come with us as a joke, Emma. I knew

(35)

she would never come. She's a child, really, and a stupid one."

"Why did you want to upset her, then?"

"I don't give a damn about her," he said. "Especially not at this moment. I know you have to leave and I don't want you to go and that is really all I'm thinking about now."

I accepted this, though I didn't believe it. He put his arm around me and we made the long dreary walk back to my house.

SEVEN

W HEN Claire went back into the rectory, she dismissed the thought of Pascal immediately. She wished she had not seen him. Instead, I later learned, she spent a few moments thinking of me. She had gone into the garden intending only to compose her thoughts after three hours of totaling lines of numbers, and when she opened the door and saw the stone white arm of Jesus raised above the azaleas in the garden, she thought of St. Thérèse of Jesus, of how, when Christ first began to present Himself in visions to her, He had begun by showing her His hands. She was sinking into a reverie, thinking of St. Thérèse's poor health and of her own state of constant blossoming. Claire felt she possessed more physical strength than was good for her. She was reproaching herself for her own reluctance to use this strength in combination with her free will, which she believed to be the most precious of God's gifts, when Pascal called her name. Now she returned to these thoughts, including in them the impression she had of my face as I longed for the shadows to swallow me, trying to elude her keen eyes. There was a knock at the side door and Father Paine, rising from his desk to open it, said, "There's your mother."

In the next moment she was looking at her mother, who hurried her. "I left a cake in the oven," she said apologetically.

Claire took up her purse and followed her into the alley. Father Paine came out behind them. He always walked them safely to the bus. Claire took her mother's hand at the corner. So childlike was this gesture that her mother kissed her cheek, drawing her nearer. "Are you tired?" she asked.

Claire drew away, shy to have the priest see her as, she thought, she really was: her mother's sleepy child. "A little," she said.

On the bus, as they rode through the Quarter, Claire rested her head against the closed window. She was more comfortable in her mother's company than in any other, for in most matters they were in perfect agreement. Her mother had agreed to the year in the world with the same reluctance Claire had felt. She believed in her daughter's higher vocation so implicitly that she saw the issue as no more than a test; at worst, a waste of time. She consented to it more readily because it meant having Claire near her, just as Claire saw the opportunity to pass a year under the same roof as her mother as a distinct spiritual advantage.

The relationship between this mother and daughter was so rare that most people who contemplated it for any length of time suspected it of being hypocritical. What they didn't comprehend was how little these two women spoke to one another concerning the subject that was uppermost in both their thoughts: that Claire was being singled out for something. Her mother was a good Catholic, though not extraordinarily devout, nor did she vex herself, as her daughter did, about the possibility that she might not measure up to the expectations of a Divine Will. She wanted no more from her religion than that it comfort her in this life and shield her from the flames of the next. She didn't make the mistake of thinking that her daughter's sanctity would ensure her own. Claire, she believed, had evidenced from birth an exceptional attraction for virtue, equating virtue with beauty even as a child. Claire pursued virtue as some people pursue vice, expecting to find in that pursuit the special knowledge that would liberate her consciousness in this life.

Claire watched the driver's brown hands, calmly steering the bus through the dark streets toward home. She pressed her cheek against the window and looked out absently as the city passed her. Now they were on Esplanade, tree-shaded and, between the yellow circles of the streetlights, perfectly dark. She had the illusion that the lights were flickering. She felt oppressed and opened the window.

"I guess the air conditioning is off so they won't waste any gas," her mother said.

"It doesn't matter," she replied. "It's not hot. I just wanted some fresh air." The air that assaulted her as she said this was not fresh, though it was cool and damp. But she sensed something in it, something fetid, teeming with life, but not life as we like to think of it; rather, full with insect and worm and vermin life, such as overtakes our own lives. Claire lifted her head and did not breathe deeply, though she had thought that she must. They came to a bus stop at which several people were waiting. The bus stopped and the doors flew open with a flapping sound, like wings. Claire continued to watch the people outside. She looked more intently, for she thought she saw something moving near the feet of a child; then, when she looked again, it was gone. There was something wrong with the child, who moved her feet back and forth, shuffling them, then turned and put one hand on a mailbox. As she lifted her face, Claire was shocked to see that she was not a child at all, but a small, intensely thin woman. She grinned at Claire, showing more gum than teeth, and pointed her finger at her own face, resting the tip of it just beneath her right eye. This eye was clouded with cataract so that it was entirely gray, and the rim was reddened and covered with a greenish slime. Claire drew in her breath and looked away, but the light would not change. She thought she couldn't look back but the woman called her name, "Claire, Claire," distinctly. She gasped and looked back at the woman, who stood exactly as she had before, but now the eye she indicated was as red as blood and behind her face there was a sudden issue of steam. Did it come from a drain? Claire put her hand over her mouth. The doors closed and the bus pulled away. Dizzy with fright, she let her head drop back against the seat and closed her eyes. They were near the park. She opened her eyes and looked at the limbs of the big oak trees that obscured the sky, and through the leaves she saw that the clouds were a sickly yellow and the moon cast a lurid light. It seemed to her, as she looked up into the branches of the trees, that they were alive with creatures moving, not busily, as squirrels move, but stealthily, in sinewy motion, and that these creatures froze the moment her eyes focused on them and pressed their gray bodies against the branches so that she couldn't make out what she saw. She could scarcely breathe. The blood drained from her face and she felt drops of sweat gathering on her forehead and on her hands. She knew at once that she was not seeing with her ordinary eyes, that she was having a vision of things as they might be. She had had such visions before. She didn't know what caused them, and it was the cause that she most feared to think upon.

As a child she had distinguished one species as coming from God and another as coming from the devil, according to how pleasant the experience was and how she felt afterward. But now she knew that it was hopeless to try to determine what God wished her to see and that it was a mistake to assume that the devil could not show her anything that might increase her faith. She resolved simply to endure this second sight, though she could not go so far as Father James had suggested and attribute her visions to nervous exhaustion or the proximity of her menstrual period. Father Paine had shown a real concern about this matter and encouraged her to describe what she saw and to communicate it to no one but him. She thought he might be searching for some way to stop the visions, but she wasn't sure. He spoke of them as a transitional condition, an idea that had never occurred to her, and he said that she might pass through this obscenely literal level of understanding God's will to something better, more direct, probably more alarming. After such a vision as she had just seen, she thought, she hoped this would happen soon. She pulled the window closed and snapped the locks in place. Her mother watched her and noted the pallor of her skin, the beads of perspiration on her forehead and upper lip. "Are you all right?" she asked.

Claire rubbed her eyes roughly with her fingertips, as if she could rub away what she had seen. "I'm fine," she said softly. "I have a headache, but it's nothing. Too many numbers."

Her mother smiled at her and touched her temple shyly. "I'll fix you some hot milk when we get home," she said.

EIGHT

I N SPITE OF, or perhaps because of, the reprimand she had given him, Pascal's father could not put Claire from his thoughts. He didn't go so far as to imagine her as a daughter-in-law, though when he brushed past this idea he conceded that it wasn't beyond the limits of his imagination. It had given him immense satisfaction to have her in his living room, to observe her simple manner and modest attire. (He wished he could have reversed those adjectives, but he didn't delude himself about her manner, in which modesty was, at best, an occasional concession to good manners.) Pascal had been interested in her, he thought, and had scoffed about her afterward with more doggedness than indignation. He decided that she must visit his family again.

These arrangements proved more difficult than he expected. Claire no longer worked at St. Mark's, and Father James suggested that she was happier now at the Cathedral, that it suited her somewhat grandiose notion of what a religious environment should be. "And it's too bad," he confided to Pascal's father, "because she is a healthy young woman with a remarkable understanding, but she doesn't put a foot down in reality unless she's forced to. And

Father Paine will let her live in a dream. He lives in one himself."

Father James didn't use the word that he knew described the territory in which Claire would consent to place her foot, because it was a word that gave him a feeling of being at a loss. He had never determined whether he thought mysticism a good thing or a bad thing. It was rare enough to be ignored and on those uncomfortable occasions when it reared its head (for example, in Claire's confessions), he combated it with an appeal to the practical, the mundane, the mortal. He said, "But we are only mortals," and this always made him feel more confident.

"She isn't satisfied," he said to Pascal's father, "being only mortal."

Pascal's father considered this wisdom. She should marry and have a child, he suggested, and that would bring her down to earth.

Father James agreed. In the end he was persuaded to call Claire's mother and issue a second invitation. It was not implausible, as one of Claire's former students was to be confirmed at the morning service and Claire would certainly wish to be there. Dinner at the Toussaints' afterward could only be an added enticement.

It was arranged, though Claire's wishes were not consulted by anyone. She consented unwillingly to go, nor could she make her advisers understand how preposterous it was for her to attend a dinner party on the second day of a three-day fast. Father James and her mother agreed that God wouldn't be offended if she broke her fast and resumed it on the following day. Father James considered fasting a medieval practice and assured her that God wanted her healthy and well fed so that He could use her for His good ends.

It was Father Paine who gave her the advice she chose to take. "Go, but don't eat," he said. "They'll all be so uncomfortable you'll never be invited again."

She smiled timidly, afraid to show how well this rebellious idea suited her. Father Paine took her hand. "You may as well resign yourself to making people uncomfortable."

"I know it," she said. "I guess I've always known it. It's a relief to have someone say it."

The priest drew his hand away. In the few weeks he had known Claire (though he had seen her briefly as a child), he had felt a new world opening up to him. He had been suspicious of her at first, but gradually, convinced of her sincerity by her willingness to comply with his direction, he had begun to think about his own salvation as a thing, perhaps, not ensured by his vocation. One evening, after having heard her confession and having advised her, as usual, against scrupulosity, he had been preparing himself a cup of chocolate when he thought he heard a sound behind him. He turned around quickly, upsetting the cocoa tin and spilling the powder across the counter, and as he turned he felt a deep intuition that somehow his fate was linked to hers and that the standard advice might not apply. Alone in his bed he prayed for the grace to direct her properly. He felt as a teacher must feel who, having taught ignorant children mathematics for thirty years, is suddenly assigned the task of teaching a young Newton. Claire was the student who would surpass him, if she was not already beyond him. He shuddered at the thought of this challenge.

Now he thought to make his position on this matter of

fasting more clear. "For some people," he said, "the best course is to fight what they believe themselves to be, because they do thoroughly despise themselves." He laughed. "And often with good reason."

"I don't despise myself enough," Claire replied.

"You're proud of your virtue," he said. "There's no vanity in that."

"You don't think it's just stubbornness?"

"No," he said. "Go to the dinner and keep your fast. Father James will be unhappy, but there's nothing to be done about it."

Claire sighed. "I suppose not."

Father Paine stood up, ending their interview. "You should try not to take too much pleasure in making him unhappy," he said.

Claire smiled. "That'll be hard."

"Why should God be offended by any little pleasure you can get from doing His will?"

Claire looked up, surprised by this remark, and met her confessor's gaze. There she saw that he had not been serious and that his affection for her was clouded with fear for her. She thanked him, left him, and went out into the street. It was five in the afternoon and she had eaten nothing since six o'clock the previous evening. She walked along Chartres Street toward her home, aware of aching fatigue, of the desire, but not the energy, for prayer.

The next morning, Claire woke up at five, an hour earlier than her usual time. She lay in her bed, curled up on her side, and gazed at the crucifix on the opposite wall. It was a gift from a school friend who had entered the convent with her but had left scarcely two months later, because, she complained, she could no longer make herself pray.

Claire thought of their conversation on this matter, of how she had tried to convince her friend that the difficulty she was having might be temporary, might be a test that, once passed, would leave her stronger, more confident of having made the right choice. The religious vocation was certainly the hardest, Claire maintained. It was supposed to be hard. It was the best, the very best thing one could do. But she had argued in vain.

She allowed her eyes to rest on the figure of Christ. She thought of her fast, of what a remarkably easy thing it was, and of how it cleared her head and made her feel more alive, more intense, than she felt when she got up and set her body before a plate of food. She thought she would have a cup of tea later, that it would be refreshing. She began her morning prayers but her mind wandered. She dreaded the day she was about to enter and was excited by its prospects, all at once. It was laughable that the small sacrifice of allowing herself to be thought an obstinate, proud girl by people who neither knew nor cared for her should weigh so heavily in her prayer; she had literally to plead for the courage to do it. As she thought of her own vanity she became confused and gave up her prayer.

She sat up in bed and resolved to spend an hour doing no more than examining her own conscience and begging God's mercy for her inadequate skill at that simple task. She knew when she was perfectly convinced of her own unworthiness and when her will was so befuddled that she could not trust herself to have a good thought, a good intention; then she would find the serenity of spirit that would pull her through the long day ahead. She leaped from the bed and knelt beside it, throwing her arms out before her.

Waking up, she thought, was like being born. She had a sure sense that she was equipped to make the long journey that would end in a union with her Creator; she believed she had been sent away from Him precisely for this purpose, to see if she would come back of her own free will. Sometimes, she thought, she must look to Him like a hound for whom He held a great affection, threading her way back home, giving in to distractions, hopelessly fascinated by others of her own kind, but finally, by a confused effort of her intelligence (which He knew she never exercised to its full capacity), arriving at the door of her rightful home. Instantly the stupidity of this comparison struck her and she cast it away, opening her eyes and turning her face so that her cheek rested upon the sheet. Every day, she reflected, she woke up at sea and had to rush about getting her bearings, determining how far in which direction she had drifted in the night. She jumped to her feet and went to her dresser, pulling her white gown down to her waist as she went. She knew a sure cure for this difficulty in concentrating. She drew from the second drawer a small leather strap, fringed at one end so that the thin strips of leather fell together as she pulled it across her palm. She took a step back from the dresser, holding the edge of it with one hand while with the other she swung the strap across her side so that it snapped the long thin strips sharply across her back. She continued this, reciting in a soft, breathless voice the greeting the angel gave to Christ's Virgin Mother. Her face was innocent of expression. The little whip punctuated the prayer with sharp cracks as it began to make thin red stripes on the white skin of her back. Then she stopped, as abruptly as she had begun, and laid the strap atop the dresser, thinking to wipe the flecks of blood from it after she had finished her prayers. She returned to her knees, this time propping her arms on the bed and resting her forehead against her folded hands. The sun was just rising, and as she opened her eyes and dropped her arms before her, light streamed in through the window, illuminating the room. Her hands seemed extraordinarily white. A bird was singing urgently, but there was no other sound. The scent of starch in the sheets and in her white gown rose to her and filled her with a sense of such security that she found herself unable to focus on her own inadequacy, the thought of which had nearly overcome her, for everywhere now her imagination was filled with light and hope, and she fell back on her haunches, bringing her hands over her eyes and sighing, as she fell, "Ah, I love you. I love you." She remained silent in this awkward position for a long time and toward the end her muscles began to tremble from the strain, for she held herself rigidly. When at last she came to herself and tried to get up, her legs were cramped and she crawled on hands and knees to a chair, where she sat composedly, drawing her nightgown back over her shoulders.

In this way Claire prepared herself for her second interview with Pascal.

NINE

PASCAL prepared for the dinner party by not thinking of it at all, or this, at least, was how it appeared. He had been interested enough by Claire's combination of reticence and resolution to consider the idea of an evening in her company not entirely unpleasant. He was always pleased to see his mother, but the combined forces of Father James and his own father might, he felt sure, make him wish he had gone anywhere else. He passed the morning in the courthouse records office, tracking down a title on a piece of property he had never seen. He met me, as we had arranged, in the bar of the hotel where we sometimes passed a few hours on those occasions when we both had time and money.

I was sitting in a leather booth near the door, and as I saw him coming in my heart contracted. He was not smiling, as he often was when we met; instead he looked serious, tired, irritated. Though there had been no discernible change in our sexual relations, except for an intensification of my own desire (I wanted more, and more often), I had detected a certain weariness in his attitude toward me that worried me. The kiss he gave me as he slipped into the seat beside me was, I thought, perfunctory.

"Is something wrong?" I said.

He frowned. "No. I just had trouble getting here. The buses are getting worse every day, and with the garbage strike it's not only slow but it smells all the way."

"You should get a bicycle."

"I know it," he said. He took my arm and began to press his thumb and forefinger against the bone of my wrist. Here was a situation I had never anticipated. His desire for me agitated him so that he was annoyed by it and impatient with me.

Outside, the drizzle turned into a downpour. "How long do you have?" he asked. I rarely had more than two hours, sometimes as little as forty-five minutes to offer him. But that day I had hurried and schemed and arranged everything so that no one would require me for the whole afternoon.

"I have to be home at six-thirty," I said.

He raised his eyebrows but continued to study my hand. Then he smiled slowly, to himself. "That's not bad," he said. "I might even go so far as to say that's very good."

"What about you?" I said.

"If I make a phone call . . . two phone calls." He brought my hand to his mouth, brushing the knuckles back and forth against his lips.

"I thought," I said, "that since we have so much time I could pretend that everything you do doesn't arouse me unbearably."

He pressed his tongue between the clenched fingers of my hand. He was, I could see, genuinely pleased, already excited. "I'll go make my calls," he said. "And check in. Do you think this bar would supply us with a bottle of wine to take to the room?"

"Go ahead," I said. "I'll take care of that."

When he was gone I took two long swallows from my glass of bourbon and allowed the sweet sensation of enough time in an agreeable space to wash over me. In the pale light from the street, the bar itself was a pleasant sight. The glasses, stacked against the dark wood, glittered feebly; the great mirror, before which the bartender stood quietly slicing a lemon, seemed to have lost its power to reflect and become opaque, like dark metal. The French doors to the street stood open, and the comforting sound of the rain filled the air, making everything drowsy and cool. I anticipated the hours to come, the spacious room, the wine we would drink sitting side by side on the wide, comfortable, unfamiliar bed, our bare feet pressed into the carpet. How we would talk, quietly, anxiously, as if to get it over with so that we could get on with the more amiable business of kissing open-mouthed and then stretching out across the bed for hours of teasing, rising, falling, and rising again.

After intoxicating myself with these fancies, I went to the bar and learned that wine was not available, though, for an exorbitant price, I could purchase a bottle of bourbon. How often, I thought, had we enough time together to consume, without hurry, even a few drinks? I purchased it and turned just as Pascal came through the thick glass doors that separated the bar from the hotel lobby. He was holding a large room key in his hand.

We went to the elevator, down the thickly carpeted hall, and into the room. He shoved the door closed behind him with his foot, reaching forward, in the same motion, to catch me by the nape of my neck. Why, I wondered, as I turned to meet his embrace, was my heart pounding so

(51)

absurdly? As we kissed, he forced my mouth open so roughly I was in fear for my lips, but I didn't pull away; rather, I wrapped my arms and legs about him tightly. When he released me a little and held my face just beneath his, I noticed with a thrill that his upper lip was pulled slightly back over his teeth, as if he were about to snarl, and his eyes had a peculiar glazed look, a look in which I found myself perversely objectified; desired not for my charm or wit or grace, but for my bones and muscle and most particularly, as he sometimes confessed, for my blood.

He wound his hand through my hair, pulling it tighter and tighter so that I was unable to move my head or look anywhere but into his eyes. I brought one, then the other foot back to the floor. I could feel some of my hair coming loose in his hands, but I said nothing. I remembered the expression on his face when he had come through the bar door, and that memory made me wish to unsettle him. I unbuttoned my blouse, keeping my eyes lowered. Pascal let go of my hair. He took my face between his hands. "Look at me," he said softly. I looked and saw returning to me an expression as perplexed and curious as my own. I have always thought that when strangers exchange even the most furtive, hurried looks, worlds collide. More and more, in the days to come, I was to see in Pascal's eyes the aftermath of that collision, my world and his, coming apart. He held my eyes as he removed my skirt. Then he put his hand between my legs and pushed his fingers deep inside. I closed my eyes and sighed, dropping my head back and offering him my throat. But no sooner had I done this than my head was pulled forward. Again he wound his free hand through my hair, tighter and tighter. "Open your eyes," he said.

I obeyed, though it was difficult. I knew what there was to read in my eyes and in my posture, for my knees had weakened and my body sagged against his, my weight helplessly centered over his prying fingers. I caught his shoulder with one hand, trying to hold myself up. He smiled. "How much longer can you hold on to that bottle?" he asked.

In fact my fingers were locked around the neck of the bourbon bottle with such force that the knuckles were white. I had completely forgotten it. We both watched my hand as I loosened this death grip and the bottle fell heavily to the carpet. Pascal then began slowly removing his fingers from inside me, a process that caused me to sigh and to fall against him, both my arms circling his neck, and my face, at last, hidden against his chest. Then he lifted me easily and carried me to the bed.

Later, when his excitement was as breathtaking as my own, his mouth pressed against my shoulder and he took the flesh beneath my clavicle between his teeth. The pressure was slight at first, too slight, I thought, so I brought my hand to his neck and pressed him hard against me. There was no need to speak; he understood me, and his teeth closed more and more tightly, but still I held him there. He lifted his head and glanced at my face. "Am I hurting you?" he asked.

"No," I said, "not at all."

He gave me a quizzical look, then returned to biting me. This time he moved down a bit so that he took in the soft skin at the top of my breast. The mark his teeth left there took several days to fade and I was at some pains to hide it from my husband.

Sometimes I thought my passion for Pascal was an illness

from which I couldn't be cured. It was something to which I gave in as it swept over me, as one does to an onslaught of high fever, lying back, breathing deeply, slowly, in and out, drawing painful air over dry membranes. At other times I thought I sensed some diminishment of it, and when this happened, I held out some hope for myself. When he struck me as insensitive or absurd, as he did often enough, I thought, Remember this the next time you think too well of him.

But I never could, especially when we were alone in a room together. And how often, I think now, did I close the door against the outside world, where he might humiliate me, embarrass me, neglect me, with a sense of gratitude and no regret for anything that happened there, as if it had never been. It has always been difficult for me to weigh the value of private against public communications. I've known men, and women too, to whom a private communication has no value at all; one could have a personal and moving conversation (or something more) with such a person and find, the next day, that it was public property. I don't think such behavior can be explained simply as a lack of discretion. I think, in such a case, experience is weighed on some other kind of scale. But with Pascal I was confident that what passed between us when we were alone was ours alone, and there were times when that confidence made me so bold I blushed to see him the next day.

Sex, I thought, is a great leveler, the action by which some of us most clearly define our own character. For others, I knew, it is only another performance, an act they engage in with a good deal of apprehension and as much theatrical ability as emotional conviction. I believed myself to be in the former group, which made me more vulnerable. The whole enterprise was so dangerous, from start to finish, I thought it quite a wonder that people worked up the courage to do it at all.

But that afternoon, in that hotel, I remember clearly that we were nothing if not courageous. It was nearly dark when we emerged from the room, retraced our steps along the hall and out the French doors that led to the street. Everything was still shiny from the rain, though the sky was clear. We parted on the street, kissing briefly, exchanging promises for another meeting. I walked to the bus and rode back through the Quarter. I would be home five minutes ahead of my most ambitious schedule.

Pascal went in the other direction, toward the lake. On the bus he closed his eyes and breathed deeply. It was a long ride to his father's house, and by the time he stepped down onto the pavement near the house where he knew he would, at least once, bite back his disagreement and contempt, he resolved to put a good face on it. Oddly enough, for that evening the best face he could put on it was Claire's.

TEN

I T WAS not until they were on the bus to the Toussaints' that Claire told Father James she intended to continue her fast. She had decided that because he would doubtless rave and abuse her, it was as well to put it off, and she had the dim hope that he would be too proud to make an issue of it in front of the Toussaint family. She wondered if Pascal would be there and, if forced to take sides, which side he would take. She imagined that his distaste for the priest would make him defend her, which amused her, as she was certain he wouldn't be able to approve, or even understand, the reason for her obstinacy. He would be glad enough that she was obstinate. Throughout the Mass she had prayed that she would not insult anyone or say anything that could be misinterpreted, but as she followed Father James's wide unyielding back up the steps and into the bus, she felt that she would have done better to pray for something abstract, like world peace. This made her smile, and Father James, turning, observed it and asked her what amused her.

"The trouble I take on my own account," she said. And then she told him, as honestly as she could, why she didn't intend to break her fast.

His face reddened, and if she had taken his wrist in her hand, she would have found that his pulse raced dangerously. But he said little, saving, Claire imagined, the full expression of his rage for a more sympathetic audience than the bus, crowded with weary churchgoers, offered him. When they arrived at their stop, Claire alighted ahead of him and didn't see the look of annoyance he gave her. They stood side by side on the pavement and the hot humid air enveloped them, making it difficult to speak.

"Have you told your mother about this?" he said.

"No, Father." Claire kept her eyes down, but not from modesty. They began the short walk to the Toussaint house.

"I promise you, she will hear about it," the priest warned. "And she won't be pleased."

"Yes, Father." Claire reflected that her mother was one person she need not fear and for that mercy she was grateful. She looked up to see Mr. Toussaint standing on his screened porch, waving at them anxiously.

Pascal was sitting on the couch, and when Claire and Father James came in, despite the dagger looks his father threw at him, he didn't get up. His eyes were level with Claire's breasts, which rose and fell softly beneath the dark blouse. He couldn't make out if she wore a bra or not, and he smiled as he thought of how he would touch the center of her back at some point to set this question at rest.

It was a large party: Jean was there with his wife and young son, an ancient uncle, who was kindly, sprightly, largely deaf, and who appeared content to watch the street from his chair near the window, Pascal, Mr. and Mrs. Toussaint, Father James, who introduced Claire to the members of the party she had not previously met, and Claire. Mrs. Toussaint offered drinks before dinner. Father

James would have a small glass of wine, which, he and Mr. Toussaint agreed, was beneficial to the digestion. Pascal and his brother helped themselves to beer. Jean's wife and baby disappeared into the kitchen in search of apple juice. Claire asked for a glass of water. As she took the perspiring glass from Mrs. Toussaint, Pascal noticed that her hand trembled.

Father James noticed it as well. He interrupted Pascal's father to point this out to Claire, and he informed the company that it was the result of a "stubborn fasting which this deluded girl has told me she intends to carry on throughout the meal."

Pascal would have laughed, but his eyes met Claire's and in a look she asked him unmistakably to take her side. He settled his eyes on Father James's straining shirt front and remarked, "One can see at a glance that such a course to sanctity has never found any credit with you."

Father James ignored this remark. Instead he turned to Mrs. Toussaint, who stood in the door holding an empty tray. "I know you can dissuade her from this foolishness," he said. "If not with good sense, then with a pass through the kitchen, where, I think, those wonderful smells are coming from." As he said this there was a gathering of saliva at the corner of his thick lips. Both Claire and Pascal noticed this and exchanged horrified looks. Claire was thoroughly exasperated. There was no way now, she saw, that she would be allowed to carry out her resolution without offending Mrs. Toussaint, and she had no desire to do so. But this lady came to her rescue.

"It's hard enough to keep a good resolution," she said. "I wouldn't want to make it worse by pretending to have feelings I don't have." Then she addressed Claire, who was still too perplexed to know where she could safely rest her eyes. "It won't offend me if you don't eat," she said.

Father James, unable to think of a suitable reply, turned back to Claire. "Well, don't sit next to me," he said coldly. "I'm sure your stomach will be growling and I don't want to hear it."

Pascal wondered at the extent of the priest's distaste for Claire. He had himself been rude to Father James for years, purposefully, doggedly, but he had never earned such a venomous look as this. Though he was certain she had not failed to notice it, Claire showed no interest in it, but raised her eyes to Pascal's mother and said, "Thank you." Then she moved away from Father James and took her seat where she had taken it on her last visit. Pascal joined her at the little side table, but before he took his chair he stood facing her a moment, as if he might speak to her, but then, thinking better of it, sat down. He leaned toward her and inquired, "Isn't it a sin to go against the express wishes of one's spiritual adviser?"

"I have more than one adviser," she said. "And they aren't in agreement on this matter."

"So you choose the one that suits you?" he said. "Or are you obliged to take the most disagreeable advice you can find?"

"I'm obliged to use my own judgment," she said.

"But how will you know you're right?"

"I won't know," she said.

Pascal considered this. "Suppose several reliable religious leaders said you were wrong and one said you were right?" he suggested.

"That would be of more interest to them than it is to me." She smiled when she said this and looked up at Father

James, who sat on the couch, vehemently slapping his pants legs, which were, he maintained, inexplicably covered with animal hair.

Pascal said nothing, and eventually, without looking back at him, Claire continued. "It's not a sign from God if a good many people think I'm in the right," she said. "That's a sign from other people."

"Do you, in fact, receive signs from God?" Pascal asked.

"I don't really know," she said, turning to him. Her manner was disarmingly friendly. "But I know that should I receive any indication of His will in this life, it would come from within. It always comes from within."

"Within what?" Pascal said impatiently.

"The understanding." She raised her eyebrows, as if she had made a joke.

Pascal at that moment could think of nothing but the fact that her eyes were wide, that the irises were such a disturbing shade of gray, too light to be called gray and flecked with violet, and that the lashes were thick, though not dark, as they swept down, then up again, so that the pupils seemed to vibrate beneath them.

"You talk nonsense most affectingly," he said, leaning toward her.

She bit her lower lip and drew away. He saw that she had been excited by their conversation and that his last remark had cooled her like a slap of icy water. She stood up, nervously glancing about the room at articles of furniture; then she went out, without speaking, to the kitchen.

Pascal didn't follow. He told himself that in spite of those promising liquid eyes, the girl was a half-mad idiot.

He was not so disgusted that he didn't make certain of a seat next to this delusionary at the dinner table. Mrs.

Toussaint removed the plate from Claire's place and offered her the one thing she did allow herself, a cup of tea. Pascal saw his mother's face as she leaned over Claire's shoulder, and he realized that these two women had developed, in a few moments' time, a thoroughgoing sympathy. That Claire could recognize his mother's worth, Pascal thought, was a point in her favor. The clatter of dishes and voices that then ensued gave him the opportunity to draw her out. He wanted to talk about the evening he had seen her in the garden and he wanted to make her as uncomfortable as possible. After a moment's thought he said, "Why did you run away the other night?"

"I beg your pardon?" she replied.

"The other night. By the Cathedral."

"Oh, yes," she said. "Did I run away?"

"Don't you remember?"

"I remember going in because it was late."

"But you'd only just come out."

She lifted her cup to her lips and sipped the hot tea calmly. When she put the cup down she sighed a little, as if she were about to undertake something tiresome. "Actually," she said, turning so that Pascal would have her full attention, "I had gone out in hopes of a few minutes alone, and when I found you there I was so unsettled that I forgot myself and went back in."

Pascal noticed that she was avoiding any mention of his companion. "The woman I was with was interested in meeting you," he said.

Claire returned her attention to the tiny clear pool of her tea. "What was her name?"

"Emma," he said. "Emma Miller."

"And why was she interested in me?"

"Because I am, I imagine." Pascal delivered this pronouncement with such a soft conspiratorial inflection that Claire couldn't miss his intention and she blushed accordingly, though Pascal was mistaken when he assumed that she blushed from pleasure.

"You would do better," she said, "to take an interest in yourself."

"I thought you Christians disapproved of self-interest," he observed.

"I can't speak for all Christians," she said, "but I understand that it is possible to lose one's self-interest in prayer, and that one can best engage in that activity by becoming acquainted with oneself."

"How interesting. How unlike my father, who only prays for my conversion."

Claire smiled. Pascal's father was, at that moment, absorbed in Father James's voluble description of the backup in the rectory's sewer system. He had reported it to the city with some hope, though it was understandable that public buildings, which were backing up all over town, would receive priority treatment. Pascal's father glanced, now and then, at Claire and his son. Their inaudible exchanges, he noted, were flowly freely, an observation that made him uneasy.

"There's prayer and then there's prayer," Claire said.

Pascal pretended surprise. "You think God prefers one kind to another?"

"Of course not," she said. "How would I know anyway? All I meant was that some prayer is little more than a routine, and some makes a great effort to rise above routine."

"And God prefers the latter, obviously."

"Why would God have a preference? He loves equally."
She threw her hands out in a circle, then drew them in.
"He puts out love," she added, "as the sun puts out light.
Some people choose to encounter that light. Others don't."

"They don't," he said, "because it's a bother."

"Yes," she agreed. "I guess that's it. It is a great deal
of trouble. But I wonder how people can be so sure it's
not worth the trouble. I suppose they don't consider the
reward."

"What is the reward?"

She ignored this question. "It wouldn't do if anyone
could have it just by being curious about what it is, you
see."

Pascal persisted. "What is the reward?"

"In the next life?" she said. "Eternal life."

"But what is it in this life?"

"In this life?"

Pascal expected her to say that there was no reward in
this life; that this life was a vale of tears and suffering.
He leaned forward to catch her words.

"I suppose it's ecstasy," she said.

"Religious ecstasy." Pascal smirked. "I always think that's
like masturbation."

Claire smiled. "It would be for you, since you believe
yourself to be utterly alone."

It was precisely Claire's ability to speculate in this way,
without concentrating on anyone who might join her, that
made her so hard for Pascal to resist. It was tedious to talk
about nothing but God, but, as it is sometimes with people
who talk of nothing but sex or nothing but astrology, the
conversation often had levels that were unexpected and
fascinating. Pascal didn't feel himself endangered by her

fanaticism; he knew himself to be beyond all appeal. Indeed, he sometimes imagined the ease with which he could have turned his back on the actual scene of the crucifixion and maintained with his sensible friends that the world was improved by the death of another evangelist. He believed in a healthy skepticism and had never encountered the philosopher, in his reading or in his travels, who was so skeptical that he considered the scope of his cynicism unhealthy. Claire, he thought, was a naïve, brainwashed, mildly hysterical little chit, but she possessed two qualities he valued: she was calm in the face of ridicule, and she was impatient with hypocrisy.

For Claire's part, conversation with Pascal was something she could have done without. At that moment she preferred it to conversation with Father James, and she didn't feel herself in danger of any compromise greater than enduring Pascal's occasional rudeness, which she took to be entirely defensive and caused by his inability to ruffle her in her own defense.

They continued their conversation, neither persuading the other of anything, until dinner was over and Jean's son, kicking at his highchair, began to call for outdoor recreation. "Swing, swing," he cried, to his grandparents' amusement. The party rose, though not all at once, and began to make their way through the kitchen and out into the warm, green backyard.

Claire stepped onto the lawn ahead of Pascal, and as the breeze lifted her hair, he imagined that he caught the scent of the damp, pale neck it exposed. She turned to him, about to speak. Her lips trembled and the slant of her light eyes was more noticeable, Pascal observed, from this angle. She was looking back at him with an expression of sensuality that troubled him and he strained forward to make sure he wouldn't miss what she was about to say.

But she never said it. Pascal's brother, who stood far ahead of Claire near the back of the yard, shouted. Instantly all eyes were fastened on Jean's face and, seeing that he was not able to speak, then followed his horrified gaze. There they saw the answer to the question. Jean's baby stood among the exposed gray roots of the family oak. That he was standing quite securely was not entirely without the power to make them marvel, but just at his feet was something more marvelous, the rapidly and relentlessly advancing head of a large black snake.

Pascal shouted too and leaped forward, nearly colliding with Claire. But she had moved out of his way in the same moment, bending down, he saw, to pick something up from the grass. As she rose and took aim, Pascal passed her and he felt the breath of air disturbed by her arm as it moved back, away from him. The child was delighted, smiling, and Pascal could see the snake rising up and then, curiously, pulling back, not as if to strike but as if struck. The black head continued backward, bringing the long body with it, then fell, gracelessly, leadenly, with a dull thud, against the earth.

It was several moments before Pascal understood that Claire had picked up a rock, thrown it at the snake, and hit it on the head with enough force to stun it. He knew at once that something extraordinary had happened, and strangely, he knew that she had been responsible for it. He had turned in his flight and seen her face at the moment when, he thought, she must have known she had hit her mark. Her expression amazed him, for it was the satisfied look of a hawk who can turn and glide and perform all sorts of miracles against the laws of gravity, but thinks little of it, having been from birth, from before that, designed to do no less.

He turned back and saw his brother bring a shovel down across the head of the snake, raising his arm high as he struck a second blow, which severed the head entirely from the sinewy body. Blood oozed from the wound, and the child, who had never understood the evil nature of the beast, sat down hard on the tree root and began to scream. Jean picked the snake up by its tail and swung the long bleeding body through the air, releasing it so that it flew against the fence. He called to the others, who stood all frozen in a group near the house, "It's a king snake."

Pascal turned to Claire. "How did you do that?" he said.

She shrugged. "It was just lucky," she said. "A freak."

"You must have incredible reflexes," he said admiringly. He had stepped forward and put his hand out. She stepped back.

"It was an accident," she said. "Do you think it would have bitten the child?"

Pascal replied that he didn't think the snake had even seen the child. As he said this he reflected on the possibility that he was speaking to a virgin, and he thought that he had never made love to a virgin, having imagined, on those rare occasions when he knew himself to be attracted to such a creature, that it wouldn't be worth the effort. But Claire, he thought, as she brushed away a few drops of moisture that had collected above her mouth, might well be the exception to that rule.

ELEVEN

Pascal told me this story some time later, as we lay together on his bed. He was careful to disguise his interest in Claire, so that, hearing him talk of it, one would have thought he had discovered a new species of tropical plant. I listened indifferently. He fished a large pocketknife from his pants pocket and pulled from it a pair of tiny scissors, with which he began paring his fingernails. I watched him sleepily, wondering that I had never seen this handsome knife before. It had a number of blades, the scissors, a little screwdriver, and even an ivory toothpick.

"Do mine when you're through," I said.

"Fingernails or toenails?"

"Do both."

"I'll cut them very close," he warned.

"Go ahead. Cut them to suit yourself."

When he finished his own nails and had trimmed mine so close that my fingers felt preternaturally naked, I took the knife from him and struggled to open the blades. "This is nice," I said. I pulled out the largest blade, which was, I thought, for a knife of this sort, remarkably sharp. "Do you sharpen this?" I asked.

"Yes, I hate dull blades. What's the good of having a knife if the blade is dull?"

"That's true," I said. I left the knife open and placed it on the dresser next to the bed. The blade caught the light from the window and gleamed back at me. It fascinated me to look at it.

"That knife interests you," Pascal observed.

"Yes, it does," I admitted.

He took it up and pressed the handle into my palm. "Hold it," he said, "while I do this." Then he knelt down near the foot of the bed and buried his head between my legs, using his tongue and both hands to excite me. I closed my eyes and sighed, holding the knife tightly in my fist. It was silly, I thought, to get such a thrill from something so simple as holding a knife, but somehow it worked. I opened my eyes and looked at the blade, which I held near my face on the pillow, and the sight of it, combined with the sensations Pascal aroused, resulted in an orgasm that lasted many seconds. Pascal relented at last and sat up next to me.

"Outrageous girl," he said, smiling at me.

"I can't help it," I said.

He took the knife away from me and passed the flat of the blade over my cheek. Then he pulled my arms down and placed one knee in the crook of my left arm and the other in the hollow of my right shoulder. "Open your mouth," he said.

I opened my mouth, expecting to receive something other than what I got, for he placed the blade of the knife against my tongue. I opened my eyes and found myself looking up at his genitals. "Do you trust me?" he asked.

I said yes as best I could without moving my tongue beneath the blade. Then he took the knife away and threw it across the room. "The things you make me think of," he said, as if he were annoyed with himself. I lifted my head a little to take him into my mouth, pressing against him so that he would go deep into my throat. He moaned and sank down upon me, holding my head against his thighs with both hands. "My love," I heard him say. I felt about until I found a pillow, which I pulled under my head to relieve the strain on my neck.

TWELVE

SHORTLY after this I came down with a mysterious illness that lasted four days. I ran a high fever and was so weak at times I found it difficult to walk. On the first day I was better, I determined to take Chris out of the dark, air-conditioned rooms in which she and I had been confined. She was as reluctant about it as I. We both knew we should get out, but one had only to open the front door and be greeted by the glare of the sidewalk to reconsider all options. We waited until three, in the hope of a shower. There were clouds, had been clouds in the afternoon for days, but by five or six they cleared off, leaving not a breath of moisture behind. I hadn't the strength to ride a bicycle, so we agreed to take a bus to the Square, where there would be shade for me, ice cream to eat, and pigeons to feed for my solitary daughter. I left a note for my husband and we set out.

We took the bus to Esplanade and changed to another that brought us to the steps of the Square. Chris was serious, afraid we were on the wrong bus, as we had been once before. When the doors opened and she saw the trees, the cool stones, the fountain, the pale façade of the Cathedral, she broke free of my hand and ran. It was a relief to me to let her run. I had a clear view of her and she could go as far as the church with impunity. I followed her to the ice cream store, where we purchased a bag of corn for the birds. Then we crossed to the Square and she began tearing at her bag, jabbing her fingertips with the staples.

I sat on a bench nearby and watched her. Then I looked around myself. On the next bench an old man was pretending to be awake. On the bench next to his, turned slightly in my direction, her head bent so that she could read the small black book in her hand, was a woman I recognized. She looked up, not meeting my eyes, apparently unaware of being watched, then down again. The top button of her blouse was open and I noted the small black cross at her throat. It was Claire. Chris had a pigeon on her arm and began shouting at me, "Look, Mama, look, look!"

"That's fine," I said. "He's a big one." Then, because I had spoken, Claire looked at me, recognized me, and in the next moment our eyes met. She smiled uncomfortably. Would I speak to her? Her book fell closed in her lap.

I was condemned to stay. Chris would never leave the park until the last kernel of her corn had been consumed by the birds. She was for them, and for herself, at the very center of interest. I watched her abstractly, aware that Claire was standing up and moving, not, as I expected, toward the safety of the church, but directly toward me. I looked up to find her standing in front of me, clutching her purse in one hand, her black book in the other.

"We've met," she said. "In the garden. I wonder if you remember."

"Of course I remember," I said. "You're Claire."

She gave me a confused look so that I understood she didn't know why she had decided to have the conversation she evidently sought.

"Will you sit with me?" I asked.

She took my offer and found herself looking at Chris. "Is she your daughter?" she asked.

"Yes," I said. Chris was flat on her stomach, and three birds fought for a seat on her outstretched hand.

"She's very beautiful," Claire said.

I agreed with this observation but I didn't add what I felt to be the proper corollary, that the beauty of my child was the consolation of my life. Every night before I went off to my own troubled, guilty sleep beside my husband, I stood next to Chris's bed and watched, with renewed wonder, her innocent, beautiful sleep, her fair skin, the long, dark shadow of her eyelashes, the delicate pink flesh of her earlobes; this sight never failed to refresh me. Now she looked up at her mother, her face smudged with dirt, her hair awry, and then, attentive to her birds, she looked away.

"She looks like her father," I said.

Claire glanced at the wedding band on my finger. Disconcerted by the conclusions she was forced to draw, she looked down at her own hands folded over the book in her lap.

"How do you come to know Pascal?" I asked, though I knew the answer as well as she did.

"I don't know him really," she said. "His father is a friend of the priest at Saint Mark's. I used to run the cathechism classes there, but I've moved here now"—she looked up quickly at the Cathedral spires—"so I never see him."

"Are you teaching cathecism here?"

"A little. I'm doing a little of everything. The night I saw you I had been learning how to keep accounts."

"You like it better here?"

"Oh, yes," she said quickly, then, regretting what she had revealed, "I like it for all the wrong reasons."

I smiled, thinking for the first time that she was probably ten years younger than I. "I think that's always the case where preference is concerned," I said.

She gave me a wondering look. "I wish I had no preferences," she said. "Of any kind."

I thought of Pascal, of my husband, and found I agreed with her. "I don't think there's any way to avoid it," I said.

"No. It's a matter of always preferring the good. But sometimes I'm not even sure which is the good."

"I'm never sure of that," I said. She gave me a quick sidelong look in which I felt myself as she had first seen me, disheveled from Pascal's embrace. She was, I thought, as uncomfortable with that memory as I was.

"Though I am certain," I added, "that it's not Pascal."

"He's an aggressive man," she said, excusing me.

"Interestingly enough, he doesn't know it."

"I don't know him at all," she said. "And I've no interest in him." Her remark suggested that we change the subject.

"Is there a man who interests you?" I inquired.

She looked annoyed. "No," she said. "None."

"It seems inevitable," I said, "for someone as young and attractive as you are."

She gave me a dry smile. "Does it?"

"It was for me."

"I can't see how an affection for a man could help me, unless he was a very good man and interested in the ultimate fate of my soul."

"That would be unusual," I admitted.

"I know it." She looked around the Square as if to indicate the absence of such a man. "It seems to me that for any person inspired with a love of God, persons of the opposite sex represent a real danger for the soul. Which accounts, I suppose, for religious orders."

"Is that the life you intend for yourself?"

"Yes," she said. "It's useless for me to consider anything else, though now I'm under orders to do just that."

"Orders from whom?" I inquired.

"From people who are older and wiser and who have good intentions toward me. They do it on the best authority and I have no choice but to believe there's some wisdom in it that's beyond me."

"They want you to have some knowledge of what you turn your back on."

"I know it," she said. "It's not my will that resists, it's my ignorance."

"The world isn't so bad," I said, though I had told myself the night before, as I lay awake beside my sleeping husband, that the world wasn't worth living in. "It's a good thing to have a child." I looked at my daughter, who held her bag upside down now, spilling the last of the seeds on the bobbing heads of her admirers. "In fact," I said, "having a child is a miracle. It makes everything else narrow and trivial."

Claire gave me a surprised look. "Do you think so?" she said. "Doesn't it make life awfully complicated?"

Chris came running up to us, waving her empty bag. One of her shoelaces was untied and I bent down to redo it. She put her arms about my neck, nearly pulling me down onto the pavement and shouting in my ear, "They ate from my hand! It didn't hurt. I thought it would hurt, but it didn't."

"You're very brave," I said, freeing my neck from her grip. "Can you say hello to Claire?"

She looked at Claire quickly and said hello, her eyes fixed on the seat next to me.

Claire returned her greeting, then, addressing me, said, "How old is she?"

"I'm five," Chris told her.

"I beg your pardon," Claire said. "Of course you know how old you are."

"I know my house number too, and my street."

"In case she gets lost," I added.

"If I get lost," Chris said, excited now and looking intently at Claire to make sure she understood, "I'll find a policeman and tell him where I live and then he'll bring me home."

"Have you ever been lost?" Claire asked.

"No." Chris was disappointed. "But I might be someday."

"Would you be afraid?"

"No. I'm never afraid," she said. Then, "Sometimes I'm afraid."

"Me too," I said.

Claire slapped a mosquito on her knee. Her hand, I noticed, was very white, her fingers long and slender, the nails trimmed in perfect ovals. She raised her hand to brush back a wisp of her hair, smiling at Chris, who, I could see, was interested, though still shy of her. "I think what frightens me," Claire said, "is not knowing what I can do for myself." Chris could make no sense of this, but her curiosity got the better of her and she put her hand out to touch Claire's skirt. A dog passing in front of us veered suddenly into a bush, flushing out a thrashing cloud of pigeons. Claire and Chris looked up with expressions of matched wonder and watched the birds rising furiously in the air, stretching out into a long formation and circling the park once to come down gracefully, easily, only a few feet from where they had ascended.

I took the opportunity to observe Claire at close range and I could see what Pascal saw in her. She was not a natural beauty—her features were good though ordinary—but she possessed something more: real spiritual beauty. Seeing this, I couldn't seriously resent her. She was a sensitive young woman, that was clear, but she didn't have the special sense I have spent so long developing in myself, and to such futile ends; that is, the ability to tell when something is going on because of me. Yet she had the ability, which I don't possess, fortunately for myself, of causing people simply by her presence to want to do something. Often, as was the case with Pascal, people felt that she was in need of some instruction, that she was intelligent enough to be weaned from her dependence on religion. What most people failed to see was that she was indifferent to all such entreaties, nor did she bother herself about why anyone would want to change her. It amused her that they tried. And this amusement was usually mistaken for acquiescence, so that she might appear to wish to be parted from her faith.

As we sat there I thought that perhaps we had something in common. When a girl I too had nurtured a great love of God. I communicated my thoughts to Him regularly and asked for His help in forming good resolutions. I hadn't the courage for more than that. I fancied that He was always with me, though I didn't make the necessary extrapolation of looking for Him within myself. I knew my interior was not a habitation anyone would choose. I had, among the general run of souls, I thought, something de-cayed, something riddled with unpleasantness. I could feel the thing within me, my soul, and the genuine disorder of the place, its potential for havoc, made me reticent to expose it to any light.

I knew I was handicapped by this dark spiritual land-scape and that without light no healthy growth was pos-sible. I remembered once throwing myself on the cold tile floor in the chapel where I prayed, alone and at the close of day. I had watched the sunlight failing to illuminate the stained glass windows (how each figure faded from the heart outward), and it seemed to me that I was next in the great withdrawal of light. Struck by this, I threw my-self over the last rays upon the floor, but no sooner had I touched the spot where they fell than they were gone.

Nor was I ever enlightened.

As I watched Claire I hoped she would meet a better fate than mine. Chris took off after the dog, and we sat in silence for a few moments.

"It's very hot," she said.

"Perhaps we could walk down to the river," I suggested. "It might be cooler."

She agreed. We got up and, catching Chris up in the midst of her chase, walked across the Square. We crossed Decatur Street while Chris tugged at my arm and climbed the glaring white stairs that led to the river. At the top was a wide flagstone platform, littered with benches and shaded by carefully spaced crepe myrtle trees, the trunks of which look so like twisted human limbs. The effect at night was eerie but in the daytime it was a pleasant spot; one could walk down the steps on the other side right to the water's edge. Chris broke free and ran across the platform, then stopped abruptly and took one nervous step backward. She saw something that both frightened and fascinated her; I could tell by the way she stood, poised to run, and by the way her hands were clenched into fists at her sides. I hurried toward her and, seeing what she saw, stopped in awe. Claire came up beside us without speaking. I knelt down beside Chris and took her hand in my own.

Before us the river flowed sleepily, but between us and the dark water was a sight that would disturb our sleep for nights to come. There were great piles of stones, broken bits of cement, and, here and there, driftwood sticking up at mysterious angles, lodged by the continuous rise and fall of the brown tide. Upon these rocks, as far as we could see in either direction, were strewn the dead and dying bodies of thousands of rats. They lay in every possible contortion of an agonizing death, and some, still living, writhed among the stones or clawed frantically at the bodies of their companions. Their bodies were clotted with blood, particularly about the face. As I watched, one dying animal convulsed on the still bleeding body of another. He bit at his dead companion, then turned and dug his teeth into his own hind leg. Frantic with pain, he lifted his head and issued a little scream, but he had scarcely got the sound out when blood poured forth from his nostrils and his mouth as if he had been shot. In the next moment he was another among the dead.

Amid this carnage men walked. They wore city uniforms and they carried large plastic bags and shovels. Some worked alone, but many found it easier to work in pairs, one holding the bag open wide while the other shoveled in the bodies, dead and alive. They didn't look up at the few people who watched them from the platform, and the sight

of their grisly work was too unnerving to allow any free
exchange of conversation. As we stood there one man clam-
bered over the stones and spoke to another, who stood on
the platform. This man then turned to the growing crowd
and said, "It's not a good idea to stay around here. We
don't know what killed them."

People began to move away, as we did, and encountering
others on their way down, discouraged them from the view.
More city workers were chaining off the stairs that led to
the platform. Within five minutes it was impossible for
local citizens to see what we had seen.

We fairly staggered back to the Square and none of us
spoke. Chris held my hand fiercely in her own and when
we sat down again on a bench, she threw her arms around
my neck and began sobbing into my shoulder. Claire was
deathly pale, and she leaned forward, dropping her head
down between her knees, her eyes closed, breathing deeply.
"Are you all right?" I asked.

She sat up, sucking in a long breath through her nostrils
and smiling weakly at me. "Sometimes," she said, "I think
I see things. I think I know things. I think I knew that."

Though there was not a great deal of reason in this
remark, I thought I understood it. "Why was it so hard to
look away?" I said.

Claire nodded and touched Chris's shoulder, who only
looked up quickly, then returned to her weeping. "It's all
right, baby," I said. "I feel like crying myself."

"What does it mean?" Claire spoke softly, nor did she
address this question to me.

"Maybe they've come up with a really effective pesticide," I suggested. This idea, though I didn't believe it for
a moment, lifted my spirits a little. There might be an

inoffensive explanation for this mass death. But the man had said, I recalled, that they didn't know what had killed the rats.

I couldn't explain to myself the nature of my shock at the sight. I was appalled first to think that there had been that many rats alive. To see them dying in such agony aroused a series of emotions: pity to see such suffering even in creatures one can't help despising, a sense of horror at the ugliness of the animals, and a suspicion that I understood more than I wanted to understand and that this dark, convulsing underside of our rotting city would soon cause an upheaval that we could not ignore. Claire and I exchanged a look I was to see many times that summer. On doorsteps, in buses, on street corners, in groceries, everywhere they went, our citizens began to eye one another. Is something going irreversibly wrong? that look said. Is this going to be the big crunch? Will I survive it? Will you get out with me? Will you try to stop me?

Chris's tears subsided and she relaxed in my arms.

"I'm glad I wasn't alone," Claire said with a shudder.

That night I looked in the paper and watched the news reports on television for some further explanation of what we had seen. But there was no mention of it. It had not been, I gathered, of more import than a small fire at a plant five miles west of the city, or a shooting at a bar, or the breakdown of three pumping stations, which, for reasons no one could adequately explain, had stopped pumping out the filthy water beneath whose natural level our city, for hundreds of years, has prospered. There was also an in-depth report on a recent political battle that had at long last been resolved by the smallest election turnout in the history of our state. I had not, I thought guiltily, voted myself.

THIRTEEN

WHEN Claire left us that afternoon, she crossed the Square and pulled open the heavy doors of the Cathedral. Inside she hurried to her confession, for this was the hour in which Father Paine was available to hear her. When the business of her sins was concluded, he inquired into her progress with meditation.

"Lately," she said, "my mind wanders. I defend myself against myself as if someone were near me and accusing me."

"Of what?" the priest asked.

"Of being a fake. Of doing it all myself. Of thinking of no one but myself."

"And how do you defend yourself?"

She sighed. "Poorly, I'm afraid."

"Do you think you are a fake?"

"I don't know," she said. "I've seen people I believed to be fake and they didn't know it. The same thing could happen to me."

"Do you care how you look to people?" he asked.

"I don't want anyone to think less of the Church for having seen me."

"You know better than that," he said.

"I know it's wrong to think more of my appearance, but

(81)

I don't know . . ." She paused, looking for the right words. "I really don't know what I am and I don't trust myself, so I try to judge myself as others do, by my appearance."

"How can you say you don't know what you are?" the priest inquired.

"I do know," she said. "I'm completely self-serving."

The priest left her with that thought, and she went into the nave to say her rote prayers and to make, with a heavy heart, a full act of contrition. Then she left the dark church and resolved to walk the twenty-five blocks to her mother's house. In that time, she thought, she would consider what the priest had said and try to understand it.

She passed people who were shopping; another group stood together on the pavement in conversation. As she crossed Esplanade she saw a young man walking a large dog, and another man, derelict and already drunk for the evening, stumbled across her path, then disappeared into a long, dark alley between two buildings. Claire watched all this activity without feeling. She was odd and she knew it. She had never expected to be ordinary. Her education had equipped her with peculiar, some observers might have called them largely useless, skills. She was honest, she could spend long periods of time contemplating the vistas presented to her by her own small, pampered, nun-ridden consciousness, her will was strong, she was convinced that she was engaged in a battle for her soul, and she believed that she would prevail. She had understood early, simply from casual, childish observation of the adult world, that many people went to their graves burdened with a conscience they would not have gladly owned. That most people felt themselves to be odd, miscast, their lives misspent, this was clear to her as well as the concomitant irony that the very conviction of being different was often the greatest similarity one person might share with another. Of her own difference, her oddity, she rarely thought. When she did, she perceived it as unwillingness to share her experience with others and she taxed herself on this point. As she walked through the Quarter that evening she considered the experience she had shared, nearly against her will, at the river. Why, she wondered, had she spoken, why had she agreed so readily to walk to the river, why had she felt bound to two strangers afterward, so comfortable in the shared horror that she had been able to hint casually at her greatest fear: that her visions coalesced on a point in reality, that she had, if not a prophetic gift, an instinct for what was about to happen?

She shuddered as she walked, and looked behind her. It was hysterical to believe such things, she told herself, but wouldn't it be worse always to miss the signs that were there?

She felt the city contained something she must learn. She recalled how she had wept when the mother-general had told her that she must return home, that it was her mother's wish and her superior's as well. It was suggested that a vocation as powerful as hers would easily withstand such a test, that this test was not to break her resolution but rather to strengthen it. Her sensations, as she had packed her thin suitcase, were a mixture of fear and despair, for though she would have gladly left the world for the love of God, she didn't know whether she was strong enough to enter it for Him. Now as she walked toward her mother's house, she felt for the first time that she had made the right decision. The city was alive and made her alive in a way she had not expected. She was not, as she had feared, tempted; instead, she was enraged. Her intuitions were stronger, deeper; her sense of being watched by those gentle, loving eyes that wished her well, and wished her back, was stronger than it had ever been. The sight of the dying animals had shocked her as nothing ever had, with a clean, cold shock like a knife blade, a sensation that was pure, exhilarating, and in which pain and joy had been so mingled as to be indistinguishable. Through it all she had seen herself from a distant point, navigated through the streets, up the stairs, and across the platform by some sure and fatal hand, a hand that knew every channel and steered her, mindless of risk, to a safe and certain destination. "Here," a voice advised her, "and look here and here; this is what I want you to see." She thought she knew who her pilot was, but she asked herself how she could show her trust in Him. She couldn't resist the temptation to believe that her young life was unfolding before her according to some plan. Her constant prayer was for vigilance, that she would be prepared and willing to take on whatever tasks, large or small, she might be called upon to do. There was some part of her that longed for glory, that wished to rise through the ranks of God's beloved to a position of importance. To be of great use, she thought. But it was her habit to brush away such ambitious yearnings with the reflection that she would be on safer ground if she could escape notoriety. For, as she had explained to Father Paine, "I think so well of myself, I'm appalled at my own arrogance."

FOURTEEN

—

FOR MY part I told everyone I knew about what we saw on the river that day. Pascal was fascinated by my narration of the scene, but what I found most interesting was my failure to mention that Claire had been with me. There were a number of reasons for my silence regarding her, but the one that weighed most heavily was my suspicion that he would want me to speak ill of her, which I could not in any conscience have done. And if I hadn't done it, I thought further, he might accuse me of having come under her influence, which was in fact what had happened. I thought of her often, not as a friend but as a creation, like a work of art, that it would be a pity to destroy. This aura she had, the sense of her having been thoroughly and thoughtfully created, and not being, like most of us, a hodgepodge of moral confusion, would cause some people to envy her and others to abhor her. The clear possession of virtue, of right, leaves everyone uncomfortable. I myself had little virtue and no sense of ever being in the right, but I consoled myself that I was not so far lost as to think either not worth possessing.

So I didn't mention Claire. Instead I told him about the rats and about my fear that such a scene might permanently

(85)

alter my child's psychological balance. I wondered aloud whether it would be wiser to let the matter lie in silence or bring it up so that Chris's horror could be dispersed in conversation. Pascal had no patience with such talk. His theories about child rearing ran the narrow gamut from disinterest to insensitivity. He didn't appear to remember his own childhood, and nothing, save speculation about the nature of good and evil, irritated him more than talking about children. The subject, he often observed, bored him. Growing up, it seemed, was simply a matter of learning stoicism. It took me a while to understand what he meant by this but finally I concluded that this stoicism was simply a blatant refusal to put any emotional conviction he might experience before his pride.

I never tired of trying to draw him out on this subject. When I left off torturing him with my worries about my daughter, we turned to a joint rehearsal of what had happened at our last meeting, a practice we engaged in regularly, as if to make sure our mutual souvenir was agreed upon so that at other times we could say, that night, the night of the shower, the night of the enormous bed. That night, in my view, was memorable as the night of the arguments. We had disagreed on every subject from food to religion. I asked him why he had turned so silent on the latter topic.

"I was afraid you were about to make a fool of yourself," he said.

"How could I make a fool of myself," I asked, "when I was only trying to figure out what you think?"

"I don't know how you could do it," he said impatiently. "But you always do when you talk about religion."

"I make a fool of myself?" I asked. It was the cruelest

thing he had ever said to me and even as it stung my pride I wondered what he was really angry about, what we were really talking about.

"Yes," he said. "I won't take that back, so you'll just have to live with it."

There were more remarks, but the substance of these gave me cause for thought in the days that followed. I considered his great distaste for religion apart from this remark and as it was evidenced by this remark, for certainly he would have been more tolerant of my being foolish on any other subject, for example, wine or Chinese food or Freudian analysis, subjects I know next to nothing about but have been known to hold forth upon. This made me think of the more painful truth, that I did, in fact, know nothing about religion but, like most people, was fool enough to talk about it as if it were common knowledge. I recalled how often I examined my own conscience and found it on the whole no worse than most. It was true that I committed adultery quite willfully, but I didn't feel ill intentioned when I did it, that is, I detested none of the parties involved and felt sorry for all. So how could that be held against me? What a miserable place my conscience was, I thought, and I wondered if anyone else enjoyed such elegant hair-splitting as I did when I entered the dull parlor where I sat in honest judgment of myself. My honest judgment had been, for some time: not so bad, not so good, but no worse than some. Pascal's remark made me see that I made more excuses for myself than I deserved, that quite possibly I made a fool of myself most of the time and admired myself for the energy with which I did so.

A few days later Pascal taught me this lesson again and in such a way that I couldn't dismiss it.

I realized, but only gradually, that our lovemaking was becoming dangerous. The knife was often a part of it. Sometimes Pascal held the blade against my face with one hand and pulled my hair with the other so that I could only exchange one threat for the other. Once, unable to bear the agony of having my hair pulled, I turned decisively toward the knife, expecting to feel it cut into the flesh of my cheek and braced for that. But Pascal withdrew the blade, caught me up in his arms, and held my gently while I wept with consternation.

We never talked about what we were doing. When we closed the door behind us there was often a moment in which we simply looked at each other. Pascal's look was tender, curious, solicitous, the look one gives an injured animal. For myself, I was screwing up my courage. My heart shrank within me, but I conquered it. The silence between us grew deeper and more mysterious. At last Pascal would break it with a request. "Will you take off your blouse? Will you kneel down by the couch here? Will you go and sit on the table, please?" They were simple requests, delivered politely, interrogatively, as if I might decline.

"Will you sit on the floor here, near my chair?" he asked one afternoon as we sat drinking champagne at his apartment. I was on my third glass; I had spent the first two gazing at him over the rim of my glass, speechless and increasingly content. I slipped off my chair and sat on the floor near his feet.

"Lean forward so I can take your dress off."

I rested my forehead on the edge of his chair, between his knees, while he unhooked and unzipped my dress. There were three hooks at the top and they gave him some resistance. "What diabolical things are these?" he muttered. I raised my hand to help him but he pushed it away. "No," he said, "let me do it." Then they came free, and with a sigh of victory he unzipped the back. I raised my arms so that he could pull the dress over my head. I put my head back down between his knees and waited. For a while he rubbed my shoulders gently, squeezing my neck at the base of my skull, tighter and tighter.

"Your neck and shoulders are always so tense," he said.

"Only when I'm with you," I replied.

"Is it because you're afraid?" he asked.

"No," I said, "I'm not afraid."

His hand was in my hair and his fingers began to gather in more and more of it. Once, in a similar position, he had pulled me roughly to my feet, slammed me face down across the table, and, before I could even raise myself to my elbows, he had pulled my legs apart and entered me from the back as if I were a boy. I braced myself for this possibility as he rubbed my skull, but after a moment he released me. "Get up," he said, "and go in the bedroom. I'll be there in a minute."

I did as he told me. There was a mirror just inside the door of his room and I stopped for a moment to gaze into my own eyes, the eyes, I saw, of a soul that was lost. Then I looked at my body, slowly, taking in the dark bruise on my neck, the reddish marks on my breasts, caused I thought, by Pascal's fingers. Just inside my hipbone was a small cut and as I looked at it I recalled Pascal's mouth against it and how I had patted his head as if he were a child, then, because of what he was doing with his hands, pressed him closer and closer so that when at last he turned away his cheek was smeared with blood.

And though it must seem strange that I didn't know it

before, I knew for the first time that I was beyond hope, that I was more than half in love with death.

I went to the bed and sat down. I was tired, the champagne had left me lightheaded, and my sense of expectancy made me uncomfortable, so that no position I assumed seemed right. After a few minutes I heard Pascal in the hall. When he came in he stopped and looked at me. He had taken his clothes off and I saw, to my surprise, that he didn't have an erection. He sat down beside me and took my face in his hands. He saw, I thought, what I had seen. He kissed me slowly, gently, and I fell back beneath him, expecting this gentle force to grow severe, slowly or suddenly; it was all the same to me.

But it never did. For the hour we had left he treated me as if I were fragile. He was, I found, in his gentleness as inventive and exciting as he was when he tried to take me apart. It made me strangely sad. He held me tenderly and hid his face in my shoulder. When I felt that an orgasm was upon him, I caught his hair in my hand and tried to turn his head. "Look at me," I said. At last he lifted his head and looked down at me. His eyes were filled with tears. Then he hid his face against me again until it was all over and he was still. As I held him all my sensibilities were touched by him. He was, I understood, as helpless in our affair as I.

FIFTEEN

━━

I SAW Claire again the following weekend. I didn't think it entirely an accident that we met in the Square at exactly the same time we had met before. When Chris and I turned in at the gate, Claire stood up from her bench and walked toward us. I was pleased to see her; I had hoped she would be there. During the week I had heard a number of disturbing rumors. Several people had been hospitalized with a mysterious disease; one was from my own neighborhood. Two had been released; from four to eight, the stories varied, were still hospitalized; and one, some said two, had died. I thought it not farfetched to believe that the scene we had witnessed on the river had something to do with these rumors. But what struck me as most curious was the fact that I hadn't been able to find any report, nor had I heard any rumor, which suggested that the great rat mortality we had seen was of any significance. Indeed, I could find no evidence that it had even happened.

As we returned to her bench and sat down together, I wondered if Claire's week had been as full of incredulity as my own. She gave me a sidelong glance, then directed her attention to Chris. But the glance wasn't lost on me and I saw that she was glad of my company and nervous lest she reveal it. "Has she said much about those rats?" she asked me when Chris had run off after her pigeons.

"She's mentioned them a few times," I said. "But then she mentioned that she fell off the slide at her school a few times and I can't believe she'll carry both those memories into adulthood."

"It's odd to think that if I never saw her again she would have no memory of me," she observed, looking at Chris seriously. A child, I thought, is an unfathomable creature to a girl of twenty. Claire had not yet lost the passionate nature of a child's affections but she had mastered the suppression of it for social purposes. I wondered about myself at her age and saw again, in my memory's poorly focused eye, a young woman capable of similar passions, idealistic, intent, but, unlike this new counterpart, completely absorbed in the desire for the good opinion of strangers. Claire didn't care much for anyone's good opinion, and it was my certainty of this that made her interest in me flattering. Perhaps, I told myself, a woman ten years my senior could have saved me from my present confusion. At her age, without warning or premonition, I had hurled myself into the adult world, thinking I would rise to the top of it by virtue of my indomitable will. But my will had been broken again and again, in ways I had not anticipated, until I couldn't decide which was better, the heady rush that came when I got what I wanted or the razor clarity that was mine when I lost my heart's desire and recovered from that loss.

Claire was all in herself as we sat in the afternoon sun and she couldn't try to see herself as others saw her; she couldn't want to try. That a five-year-old could meet her and forget her constituted a mystery she hadn't the penetration to solve. As we sat together it dawned on me that she had great plans for herself and that she was preparing to execute them. She turned to me as if she were about to speak, then, thinking better of it, opened and closed her mouth silently.

"Is something wrong?" I asked.

"No," she said. "I was thinking of something you said the other day, about how hard it was to look away."

"It was," I said. "I don't know why. I suppose it's because there's no satisfactory explanation for suffering."

"It's because there is an explanation for it," she replied.

"And what could that be?" I asked.

"A sad one," she replied. "It's the only way we ever learn."

"What about the suffering of children?" I asked.

"Yes," she said. "I know that's the most difficult to accept."

"There's no accepting it," I said bitterly. Claire leaned back against the bench, flinched, and then sat forward again, propping her head in her hands, her elbows on her knees. Her back was thus displayed to me and I saw three lines of brown soaked into the pale material of her blouse. I knew at once what it was and, and in that same moment, I knew how she had done it. I was shocked, though I didn't know why.

It isn't a very difficult thing to inflict such delicate wounds on oneself. I know it now, though I didn't then. The back is particularly vulnerable. A few stinging blows from an ordinary leather belt will yield welts that are disproportionately ugly to the pain of the blows. And the belt, as it whips through the air, makes a clean crack across the sparsely covered bones of the spinal column. The sound alone provides relief from frustration, particularly of a sexual nature. The relief makes the relative pain involved a matter of little consequence. Self-inflicted pain has a calming effect; it clears the head, diminishes one's fascination with the ego, and, most important, gives one the sense of having taken some real action against the everyday foolishness of the body and of the vagrant, willful, heedless imagination. But I didn't know any of this then and I felt, as I imagine many people do, that when a desire for a self-discipline results in self-abuse, it's a sure sign of a self-indulgent and excessively dramatic imagination.

"Why are you torturing yourself?" I asked, careful to keep any emotion save curiosity out of my voice, so that I sounded like someone seeking information and nothing more.

She kept her back to me. "Why are you torturing yourself?" she replied. Then, because I didn't respond, she added, "For Pascal?"

It was true, I thought. I did torture myself for him. Sometimes I even tortured myself *with* him.

Then she answered the question I had put to her. "I do it," she said, "to make up for my miserable nature, for my inability to do something so simple and necessary as caring for people who don't love me."

"And whom you don't love," I added.

"Especially for that."

"Does your confessor know this?"

"About my feelings?" she said. "Of course."

"And about the way you compensate?"

"I confess everything," she said. "I don't hold anything back."

"I should think it would be impossible to confess everything," I said. "Even if you wanted to."

"I don't see why."

"Our actions are seldom what they seem. Vanity masks itself as charity, and vice versa."

She laughed. "I follow you as far as the vice versa," she said.

"What?" I replied. I hadn't been paying attention to my own conversation. I tried to think of an example. "One could pretend to be aloof in order to spare someone else humiliation."

"The humiliation of offering you a love you can't return," she suggested.

"Yes, that would be a case."

"Is that what you think I'm doing?" she said.

"Is someone in love with you?"

"No," she said. "I believe Pascal will come to think he is. And so do you."

I looked away. I felt as though I had been stung. With all my heart I liked this young woman and I had a mental picture of her submitting to one of Pascal's more devastating caresses, a picture that developed before my eyes like a snapshot. My throat and chest ached. I couldn't answer her.

Nor did she expect an answer. After a moment she continued. "I know I'm probably the last virgin my age on the continent," she said. "It's my greatest vanity."

"But you're not tempted to give it up?"

"I'm glad to hear someone speak as if it were to be given up rather than thrown off like some nasty-smelling sweater."

"Losing one's virginity isn't all that important," I suggested.

"I don't want to lose it," she said hotly. "It's part of me. It's the best thing about me, as far as I can tell."

"Certainly you wouldn't be the same without it."

(95)

"That's just it," she said eagerly. "I honestly believe that the soul and the body are tied up together in this life and you can't be heedless of one without damaging the other."

"Then why," I said, indicating her back with a lift of my chin, "why abuse your body?"

"My body can easily take a beating, especially as it comes from my will. But I don't wish to subject either my soul or my body to the will of someone who values neither."

"I envy you," I said.

"I know," she said quietly. "I knew that the first time I saw you. You think it's too late for you, so you envy me. But I don't see that it's too late for you. There's plenty to do; there's always plenty to do. There's no end to the service you can do."

I thought of Pascal. I could taste the metallic oiliness of the knife he had once put in my mouth. I wanted him badly. "I'm sorry," I said. "It's too late for me. You may as well give up right now."

"Being honest with yourself is the first step to real virtue," she said, as if I had just taken the first step right before her eyes.

"It is *real* virtue you're after," I said. "Nothing less will do."

She looked away and I thought she did so because of an excess of emotion. "I want to go to my bed at night with a clear conscience and I want to do it night after night until it's a habit I can't break even should I want to."

"Well, I wish you luck," I said. "I'll be interested to see what happens to you."

We continued to talk. She inspired me with a sense of what I had given up in my appetite for personal relations. I saw how the ties people stretch one to another, with language and with emotion, only echo the fragility of all the ties nature forges. How far down the line a small disturbance reverberates, as if matter itself were distorted by a wave of desire, or fear, or deep longing. And it seemed to me that longing was everything, longing is all we are. We long for a life we never had but of which we seem to have a clear memory; a life in which there is no longing. Claire talked of these matters with a clarity of understanding that surprised as well as affected me. I remembered what I had felt at her age, the unendurable battles that went on in my consciousness: Would I be good or would I be pleasing, for that was the issue as I saw it then. It didn't occur to me until much too late that neither option was entirely mine to choose. I knew, as I watched Claire endeavoring to inspire in me a more pure, more divine love than any I had experienced, that there had never been much likelihood of my being good. I was too taken with the great tragedy of separation I saw everywhere around me to want to end it in myself. I wanted to be separated from God; it suited me. Claire wanted only to be reunited, yet we sat and talked of the dangers of scrupulosity, the proper attitude to take toward those people one failed to love, the nature of evil, as if we spoke the same language. I knew I was lying to her and that it was a self-serving lie, but I couldn't stop, nor did I warn her that I was not to be trusted. I judged that thinking well of me would do her no harm.

In return for my wisdom, Claire narrated many of the events of her life so that I might understand and approve of the manner in which she had arrived at her resolutions. She had imagined for some time that true happiness, which she equated with a proper understanding of one's vocation (and who can dispute such a simple equation), lay behind the convent doors and nowhere else. This was partly because her experience with the outside world had ended while she was still a child and partly because the convent life provided her passionate spirit with so many checks and balances that she was even tempered only when under its rigorous rule. In her mother's house she retained as much of the convent routine as possible, rising early, reading her office, eating at specific times; she even tried to keep the regularly spaced recreations.

This was difficult, as she had always passed the time in frenzied physical exercise, usually with partners equally intent, playing tennis on the school court, basketball in the gymnasium, murderously serious baseball on the long lawn behind the cloister, or, when it rained, roller skating in the basement. Her mother's house provided none of the necessary equipment, so she was often reduced to running around the dangerous block they lived in or doing sit-ups in her cell-like bedroom.

This lonely recreation, she feared, was bad for her. She slipped out of consciousness too easily and found herself two miles farther than she had intended, or curled up on the floor of her room, her body soaked with sweat, her heart pounding torridly in her ears, her hands clasped in fists before her eyes. She didn't think she was in ecstasy during these times, though anyone who saw her a moment before she recollected herself would certainly have concluded that she was beyond the reach of reason.

One day she experienced such a lapse during her prayers in the Cathedral. She had been thinking of Christ's hand as it closed about the shank of the impending nail; then she opened her eyes to find Father Paine bending over her, his face furrowed with concern. "Can you hear me now?"

he said. She sat up on the cold floor and covered her eyes with her hands.

"Did you speak before?" she asked. He helped her to her feet, pulling her up by one elbow. Two old women sat three aisles up, completely turned away from the altar; their eyes poured over Claire's small figure with a greediness akin to lust. "I beg your pardon," Claire said softly. Father Paine steered her into a pew near the rear of the church and sat down beside her.

"What happened?" he said.

"I must have fainted."

He wasn't fooled by this reply. "What happened?" he persisted.

Claire looked hard at the back of the pew before her. "His hand," she said.

They sat in silence, nor did she raise a hand to wipe away the tears that streamed down her face. She didn't gasp, her breathing was not affected, but she wept for a few minutes while he sat beside her. He didn't touch her; in fact, he drew himself a little away. She felt this and looked up at him, her face pitiful with fear and sadness.

"I can't tell you what to do," he said.

"But can you forgive me?" she asked, her eyes imploring.

"Yes," he said. "With all my heart." He stood up and walked quickly out. Claire fell back in her seat and tried to compose her thoughts. Her efforts were futile. Beneath the superficial rote prayers, the routine avowals of faith and trust, the expressions of gratitude for the Divine Love she continually enjoyed, she could hear, clearly, her own frightened voice crying out, "Not me. Don't do this to me. I can't yield to this willingly. Why are you choosing me? What do you want from me? Why me?"

She described to me her realization that her Lover wanted

more than her service. He wanted her entirely; He wanted her soul for His own and His desire was not diminished by her fear of being owned.

Which was exactly the position I found myself in with Pascal. I was entirely desired, and willing to be so, yet afraid. I sought ways to give myself over. I employed a line of reasoning similar to one I had used as a girl to rid myself of timidity before doctors. I told myself that Pascal had doubtless seen more disturbing sights than any I might show him. And so when he looked at me I fairly preened before him and when he penetrated the secret passages of my body I gave myself up to the pleasure of being explored.

The intensity of my responses was a wonder to me. It was as if someone had opened an unexpected door, and a world I hadn't dreamed of had spread itself before me. I knew of many passionate relationships; in most it seemed to me the parties involved *spent* more passion than they felt. I had known couples who couldn't meet unless the ground beneath them was a declared battlefield. But this was different; my passion was for him, not against him, and he seemed to return my feeling. The desire to arouse desire was new to me and I found myself thinking with satisfaction, a hundred times a day, of moments when I knew I had provoked him.

But I said nothing of this to Claire, who could only have found my behavior as strange as I found hers.

SIXTEEN

I DIDN'T see Claire for some weeks after this. The city was in a condition of such overt decline that those who had been predicting it began to take heart, yet in the midst of political and social confusion, individual lives went on much as usual. Everything was inconvenient but our citizens took each new blow to the general welfare with the same cheerful resignation that for two hundred years had sustained them through the vicissitudes of the climate. It was August, the month through which we moved listlessly, but not without hope, for August was always the worst test of our communal courage. This was to be the most arduous August in many memories. It was mercilessly hot; the daylight hours were unbearable. One morning I stood on my front step and watched two young girls, one shod, one barefoot, preparing to cross the street, a small enough expanse of white concrete, though it turned back the sun's rays with such violence that it appeared to be a sheet of gleaming metal. The girls hesitated on the grass, but not for fear of cars, for there were none. After a brief consultation the barefoot girl climbed onto the back of her more fortunate friend and was carried to the safety of another patch of grass.

The sun took our breath away by day; the mosquitoes took our blood by night. They descended on our weakened resistance with the fury of an invading culture. Mothers struck their children for leaving a screen door ajar. In my neighborhood the children who could not be kept in at night ran about with legs and arms swollen with bites, some bleeding and open from their constant scratching.

Still there were a few safe, even pleasant hours every afternoon, and most people tried to conduct the important business of life in these. The rain began every day between two and three and cleared off by five. The rapidly assembled clouds shielded us from the sun; the cool rain fell softly even as the warm steam rose to meet it. The French Quarter, with its sheltered sidewalks, was the best place to be. One could walk in the cooled air and hear the pleasant sound of the water beating resolutely against tin, against concrete, against glass, everywhere with the same gentle insistence. The senses expanded, odors arrived at the nose in a liquid rush, sounds were filtered by the heavy air, eyes that had been crossed from squinting at the light slowly cleared and rested on a scene softened through a mist. On one such afternoon Pascal made his way up Royal Street, across Pirates Alley, and into the wide stone portico of the Cabildo. He paused, looking out at the Square.

Pascal was so confident of his own worth that sometimes he failed to notice it and in such moments he approached a selfless abstraction that Claire might have found virtuous. He was in just such a state as he stood looking into the rain; he desired nothing. He had arrived in plenty of time for the concert he planned to attend at the Cathedral and had stopped to admire the rain, alone, unhurried. It was as if he'd come upon a pleasant old acquaintance. He felt

awake, well invested in his senses, and believed he possessed formidable powers of mind. He had always packed
his brain with as much information as it would retain and
he was keenly aware of how superior his powers of reten-
tion were. He could, he knew, use his brain as a weapon,
and he couldn't recall that, when forced to do so, he had
ever encountered any real threats to its tactical capabilities.
But he preferred to use it passively, as he did now, as a
muscle might be exercised for the long-range benefits to
one's health. It was natural for him to relax himself in
this way and not, as others might, in idle speculation. As
a rule he disliked speculation because he believed that it
could never eventually lead to the truth but only some
crass approximation of the truth. I was never able to determine whether he thought some other route might lead
to the discovery of anything more tangible, because whenever I complained of the uselessness of my own meta-
physical systems, he gave me a look of the coldest indif-
ference, as if I had just mentioned something so distasteful
it had caused him to wonder if I were sane.

If he thought there was some way of getting at the truth,
or if he believed there was even an unwavering truth to
be gotten at, I don't know. He gave such questions no
thought, at least, as he stood in the wide portico of the
Cabildo and looked out into the rain. His hands hung limply
at his sides, his eyes scanned the simple scene before them
with kindly interest, and he sighed. The corners of his
mouth drew up a bit in this sigh so that he seemed to be
remembering something pleasant as well as something ir-
retrievably lost. He could hear hurried footsteps on the
sidewalk behind him, someone running along the side street,
where there was no cover, in a hurry to get under the

shelter he now shared with no one. He didn't turn when he heard the steps change both their speed and their tone as the heels passed from the concrete to the wide smooth paving stones. He felt that it was a woman — the step had been light and quick — and he hesitated before turning to look at her so long that he thought another moment would be the one in which it became rude to do so. She had stopped and was standing perhaps twenty feet behind him, in the darker shadow of the building. His first thought on looking at her was relief, for she was not looking at him; in fact, she hadn't seen him, so engrossed was she in examining one of her shoes. This article she had removed from her foot and she was bent intently over it, pressing the small wooden heel back onto the shoe. Pascal's second thought was all recognition; he knew the woman, he knew in a glance her situation, he even imagined that he knew how the heel had parted company with the shoe.

"Claire," he said, with such an expression of surprise that she looked up from her work and took a step backward at once.

She said hello without conviction. Pascal thought she didn't recognize him, but then she smiled briefly as a signal that she owned to knowing him and accepted his right to speak to her.

"Are you going to the concert?" he asked.

"Yes," she said. Then, allowing the shoe to come apart in her hands, she added, "It looks as if I'm going in one shoe."

"Let me look at it," he said, taking the pieces from her. She explained how it had broken as she leaped from the street onto the curb, how she had gone a few steps not understanding what was wrong and had then gone back to retrieve the heel from the puddle in which it had fallen. Pascal meantime had straightened the little nails against the stone wall next to him and replaced the heel, pressing it back into place with such force as to make it temporarily operable.

"You've fixed it," she said on receiving it.

"Not for long, I think," he said. "Be careful how you walk on it."

She placed the shoe on the pavement and slipped her foot into it. Pascal noticed the fineness of her ankle, the deep arch of her foot. She was wearing stockings of a pale heavy material, too heavy, Pascal thought, for the heat of the day. She put her weight upon the shoe, and the heel, a wide low heel that was not entirely unfashionable, held. She straightened up, smiling at Pascal with genuine gratitude. "Thank you," she said.

"We're early," Pascal said with a significant look at his watch. "Would you like to get some coffee?"

"I came early on purpose," she said. "I like to pray before hearing music." She said this simply, without any particular emphasis, as if it were an ordinary thing to do, like washing one's hands before eating. Pascal couldn't keep his eyes from rolling upward a little with incredulity.

"Don't you pray enough?" he said. "Can't you be spared a little of it for some innocent conversation?" His voice didn't convey all the sarcasm he felt; he held it back a little, for he found he wanted her to go with him very much.

"I don't need to be spared it," she said. "I do it for the pleasure of it."

"Then I suppose it's I who will be spared," he said wearily.

"You would if I chose not to go with you," she replied, "but you've made such a point of it now that I think I will. I don't want you to feel you've gotten away with anything."

"That's clever of you," he said, "but you've only rationalized doing what I want." And with that he took her arm and led her across the cold face of the Cathedral to the shelter of the Presbytère, and then hurriedly along the covered walk before the Pontalba apartments and across Decatur Street to the café. She went along willingly enough, though she anticipated more the stimulation of the hot coffee, a luxury she didn't often allow herself, than anything Pascal might offer as conversation, for she had sensed in her first meeting with him the impossibility of any encounter that would be entirely "innocent." It was a word, she thought, he had used because he imagined it would appeal to her. She recalled a priest in the convent who had tempted her friend with the argument that since she was giving up the life of the senses, she should talk to him about what she was giving up; she should think of her own sexuality and explore it in the hope of coming to terms with it, and she should tell him of her experiments. Claire had laughed on hearing this. "It's a wonderful theory," she had exclaimed. "Like setting fire to one's clothes to understand the nature of heat."

Her friend had hung her head at this remark, adding lamely, "He did say one had to get wet to learn to swim." The two had then collapsed in such helpless laughter that Claire smiled just thinking of it. Pascal caught this smile and wondered if it was directed at him.

"What's funny?" he inquired.

The smile disappeared, was replaced by a frown. "Nothing," she said. "I was thinking of something someone said when I was in the convent."

"I've never understood about that," Pascal said. "Were you really a nun or were you just a student?"

"I was a student for nine years and then I was a postulant for nearly a year before I left."

Pascal looked at her wonderingly. "Why?" he said.

They had arrived at the café with this question, and it hung on the air until they took one of the many vacant tables beneath the canvas awning and settled into their chairs.

"Why what?" Claire picked it up. "Why did I go in or why did I leave?"

"I hope you left because you came to your senses," Pascal observed. "And if I'm wrong, perhaps you'll be good enough not to tell me."

"I intend to return as soon as I'm allowed to," Claire replied. "So I suppose there's no hope of my being in my senses."

With this the waitress arrived and learned that they would have coffee only, though Pascal protested that Claire should eat a few beignets, lest a wind come and carry her away. "You are eating food these days?" he continued when they were alone again. "Or is your favorite diet still air and water?"

"I eat plenty enough," Claire said testily. "My health is probably better than yours."

Pascal smiled. The coffee arrived and they spent a quiet moment stirring and tasting. Claire put her cup away from her after the first sip and gazed at it. "That's very good," she said. "The coffee here is really so good."

Pascal would have made some observation about the degree of her pleasure in what should have been a common enough experience, but he was struck with sadness as he looked at her and so he held his tongue. Instead he had a series of reflections, some trivial—why was youth and health and a fair amount of beauty wasted on this fanatical young person?—others more personal—would she some-day see the foolishness of denying herself such simple pleas-ures as a cup of coffee could give her and would he be the one to persuade her?

"Yes, it is" was all he said, and when she caught his eye he looked away, out at the street, where the rain had turned to a drizzle and the blessed clouds were already thinning.

As he watched, Claire began to speak in such a low confidential tone that he inclined himself toward her, though he didn't take his eyes from the street. He sensed that if he looked at her she would stop talking and, he thought, he didn't want her to stop.

"I know," she said, "what you think of me. You think I'm foolish and deluded and deny myself the pleasure I could have in the insane hope that I'll be rewarded for it in some other life. Perhaps you're right, though I don't see how you could be. But I behave the way I do for another reason as well; it gives me pleasure. I like what I'm doing and I'm happy as I am. That's what you won't be able to understand about me and why we have very little to talk about." She stopped, waiting for his reply.

"I don't think you foolish," he said, turning his attention to her with a force he knew to be disarming. He looked into her eyes as he spoke and made a great effort to take as seriously as possible the calm look she returned to him. "I only think you very young and inexperienced."

"It's my inexperience that provokes you then," she said.

"You don't provoke me," he replied, nor did he think it was dishonest to say so. "I was delighted to see you. I look forward to being with you at the concert. I'll be reluctant to leave you when it's over. Does that sound as if I'm provoked?"

Claire looked away. She gave herself over to an intense dislike of him. She could think of nothing but unpleasant things to say and she rummaged among them for the least offensive. But Pascal read her thoughts and put them to her.

"It's you who are provoked. You'd much rather be on your knees over there"—he gestured toward the Cathedral—"all by yourself with your little fantasies, because then you'd feel safe and comfortable, whereas with me you think you're in danger."

"I don't see how you could constitute a danger to me," she said, "as I've no interest in your opinions."

"You lack courage," he observed.

"And you lack courtesy," she replied tartly.

She felt her temper rising and wondered if in the next exchange it might not lift her entirely out of her seat. But she had wounded Pascal instinctively in a vulnerable spot. He would take any woman as far as she was willing to go but he flattered himself that he never used force.

"I beg your pardon," he said simply. "If you want me to leave you, I will."

"No," she said, though that was exactly what she wanted, had wanted from the moment she recognized him. "I take myself too seriously." After a pause she added, "And it's true that sometimes I lack courage. But I'm not afraid of you." She gave him her full attention for this last remark and followed it with a smile that he characterized as deceptive, even sly.

"There's no reason why you should be," he replied. "I mean you no harm."

They were reconciled sufficiently to talk of something

other than the fact of their being together. They turned their attention to the sun, which was, even as they sat there, transforming a warm, rainy, intimate atmosphere into a glaring, steaming, comfortless miasma. Pascal couldn't bear the heat and said so. Claire maintained that it didn't have a bad effect on her. Then, as they looked out toward the river, she began to tell him about the day she had seen the dying rats. She spoke as if she expected him to have some knowledge of it, which he did in fact possess. But his surprise at learning that she had been in my company was so great that he became excited and interrupted her.

"But Emma didn't tell me you were there," he said. "She didn't mention you at all."

"Didn't she?" Claire replied dreamily. "I can't think why she wouldn't."

"I can think of a good many reasons," he said. "And none of them are flattering to her."

"It was a chance meeting," she said. "And I went away right afterward." She said this as if it explained my silence on the subject, though she saw at once that it explained nothing. She wondered how Pascal had made her feel defensive on the subject. "Why should she mention me?" she concluded weakly.

"Exactly," he replied. "It's as if she thought nothing of you, and her having done so convinces me that she thought a great deal of your being there."

"Must people always be disguising their real motives?" Claire asked.

"I know Emma well enough to think that her not mentioning you could have happened only if she'd made the choice not to. It's not natural of her not to mention such a thing."

Claire gave an impatient look to the chair next to her. "I certainly wish *I* hadn't mentioned it," she said. This display of exasperation impressed Pascal. He changed the subject at once, nor did he revert to it in the time they spent together, though he was to labor me about it until, in spite of the fact that my temper is milder than Claire's, I too lost patience.

They talked a little of life in the city, both expressing their conviction that something ominous was in the air. Pascal cited the facts and Claire described the emanations, so that, without either willing it, they arrived at a final picture more alarming than either had intended. At least, they agreed, the buses continued to run and there was still music to be heard. The concert they planned now to attend might be a very good one and, they learned by consulting the wide clock face on the Cathedral, it was about to begin.

Claire was more comfortable in Pascal's company on the walk back across the Square. She took advantage of this feeling to try more directly to get away from him. "I intend," she said, "to spend any time we have to wait in praying," she said. "You may prefer not to sit with me."

Pascal's sense of outrage was so inflamed by this remark that he replied, in a tone expressing the mildest interest, a tone he often employed just prior to delivering what he considered to be a crushing blow, "Will you be kneeling or sitting?"

Claire was off her guard. He could scarcely credit the open innocence she displayed in her answer. "Sitting," she said, "so as not to draw attention to myself."

"And your hands," he said, his voice harsh with contempt, "I've no doubt you'll have them in your lap?"

Claire shrank at his side. His remark so stunned her

that she was plunged into silence. Her heart began beating
rapidly. Her breath shortened and her head rang. They
had arrived at the steps of the Cathedral, and Pascal, taking
her elbow, guided her up and across the narthex without
either of them speaking. Inside the nave Claire came to
herself and pulled deliberately away from him. It was impossible to speak now. The little orchestra struck up the
first tragic notes of Scarlatti's *Stabat Mater*, the sopranos
stepped forward to their lecterns. Claire took what she saw
to be, musically speaking, an inferior seat, on the side and
away from the crowded center aisle. There was plenty of
room, but no sooner had she sat down than she was forced
to move aside to accommodate Pascal, who sat purposefully
next her. Claire moved away from him as best she could,
refusing to meet his cheerful eye. He was pleased with
himself, though a little fearful lest he had said too much
too quickly. Claire's anger showed in her face and made
her, he noticed, charming. She tried to concentrate on the
music, which poured out lushly into the damp, cool air of
the Cathedral. Beneath the musical pathos she could hear
the delicate whirring of strategically placed electric fans.
Claire thought of what the music had been written to make
her think about: the Mother of Christ as she stood beneath
the cross on which her only Son hung in agony, still conscious, His divine eyes fixed on her. Who, born of woman,
the singers intoned, could not weep for her amazing trouble. She had been born only that she might bear it. Claire
wondered, as she thought of this, how she could find the
doubtless smaller trouble for which she herself had been
designed. This futile thinking annoyed her and she closed
her eyes, banishing everything but the mental picture of
Christ's suffering. Her hands lay clenched at her sides;

she had not relaxed her fingers since Pascal had made his crude remark on the street. Her fingernails dug into her palms. Then the music became more powerful, the voices begged to share in the passion of their Maker, and Claire's inner voice rose with them. She thought of His hands, how the broken nerves and flesh must have throbbed from the shock of the nails. Her throat contracted and from it issued a sigh, almost inaudible, such as escapes with the onset of anticipated pain. Then she was catapulted to consciousness by something unthinkable: a strong hand had taken her own and gently pried the fingers from the palm. Her eyes flew open; she was nearly in a swoon. She saw at once that Pascal had taken her hand, that he smoothed it now as he bent on her a look she couldn't but appreciate, full of concern, affection, even, she thought, a glimmer of admiration. "Are you all right?" he said softly. "Shall I take you out?"

She drew herself away, her hand away, and though he could see she was discomposed, she replied sensibly enough. "No," she said. "Thank you. I'm all right."

He continued to look at her sadly, without speaking. She hung her head, feeling, she couldn't say why, as if she had behaved so shamefully she had best leave. The music swelled to a crescendo, but neither Claire nor Pascal was aware of it. "Excuse me," she said softly. With this she stood up and went away, not crossing in front of him but slipping to the farther end of the aisle and out the rear door. Pascal watched her until she was out of sight, then turned and tried unsuccessfully to concentrate on the touching and sensuous beauty of Scarlatti's music.

He sat in dismal awareness of her absence. She had left an impression on him and though it was not altogether a favorable one, he could not think himself pitiable for having received it. It was usually enough for him to discover that a person held less idiotic views than those he knew Claire to hold to engender in him a distaste that was akin to the feeling of being set at liberty. But liberty from Claire was not what it should have been; he had liked her presence somehow, in spite of her idiocy. He hated the platitudes she mouthed; the way she spoke of wishing to pray was so absurd he had been hard pressed to keep from outright laughter. Had anyone else expressed such a wish he knew he would have laughed. Why then, he thought, had he longed not to laugh at her but to persuade her, to take her lovely empty head between his hands and press some sense into it? She had ruined his afternoon, ruined the concert, ruined his sense of well-being, of holding no grudges. For, he thought, as he looked about the spacious Cathedral, he held a grudge against all those who had deprived her of what she deserved: an unstinting and unprejudiced education.

SEVENTEEN

—

O N THE very evening of the spoiled concert, I too
became the victim of an unexpected, undesired encounter.
It was Chris's night to visit her grandmother and, after
seeing her safely there, I took the bus home. I was later
than I'd hoped, but I still had an hour before my husband
could be expected to arrive. I walked through the long,
dark shotgun house, flipping light switches on behind me
as I went. The kitchen was at the very back of the house
and as I turned on the last switch I was thinking of how
it must look from the outside, one window after another
flashing awake, like a train coming slowly out of a tunnel.

My husband was sitting at the kitchen table, and though
his eyes were squinting from the light he was looking directly
at me.

I slumped in the doorway. "What are you doing?" I said.
"Waiting for you."
"In the dark?" My heart sank. Excuses leaped to my
mind but they were like spray around a heavy stone dropped
into the water. The stone was my certainty that no lie
could disguise the truth because he already knew the truth.
I stepped into the room and stood with my back against
the stove. I'm back, my posture announced. I'm about to
cook.

He was merciful and for the small kindness he paid me by not prying a confession from me, I was grateful. "I know about this man," he said. "I know who he is and how often you see him, though I don't know exactly how long you've been seeing him."

"A long time," I said. I was struck with the way he looked; it was as if I had never seen him. His whole expression was of distrust and impatience. The lines about his mouth and his eyes revealed to me that this was not the sudden expression of the moment but that it had been set this way for some time. Only deep and obsessive brooding could have caused such a change in a face I remembered as having always been without malice. For some time I had massaged my conscience with the observation that he didn't understand me; now I saw that it was deeper still: I didn't understand him.

He knew this too. "How could you choose someone like that?" he said.

"He chose me," I replied. I thought this an intelligent reply for the first two of the five seconds it lay on the air between us. Then I saw it as a dismal species of ordering.

"If I tell you that you must stop seeing him for your own good, will you do it?"

The expression "for your own good" stuck with me. Was it possible that I didn't know my own good? I knew that, in spite of the natural tendency of all living things to choose or create those conditions which encourage longevity, it is possible for us humans to lose sight of this commodity, this "good." Sometimes, I thought, it wasn't natural to attempt to flourish. I thought of how Claire had once explained her conviction that free will was more than an idea, that for humans, alone among the animals, free will was a very unpleasant given. One couldn't give up one's free will or have it taken away, in her opinion. The option to choose what to think and how to act was ours every moment we breathed. Now my husband suggested that he had observed me continually choosing what he saw as harmful to me. I knew enough about Pascal to believe that he was unlikely to be good for me, for my peace of mind, for the long stretch to the grave, so, I thought, it was possible that my husband was right. I disliked him so much for having suddenly stirred up these doubts that I said, "No. I wouldn't."

"Then you've made your choice?"

"No. You make it. It's your choice."

He put his head in his hands for a moment, a gesture characteristic of despair. I noted my lack of sympathy with this gesture. Get it over with, I thought. He looked up. "I won't leave Chris with you," he said. "You can't have her."

Why hadn't I prepared for this? I thought. Hadn't I known where the field of battle would be? I pleaded for reason. "We can't bring her into this. She can't be a weapon for us. She doesn't deserve that. She shouldn't even suspect that we don't love each other. We'll just have to pretend we still do."

"I don't have to pretend," he said. "I do love you."

This remark threw the responsibility back to me and he continued to use it as a defensive tactic in the days to come. The entire blame, in this way, was placed on me. He even went so far as to say that he didn't blame me, that he could see he had taken me for granted and would not do so in the future. He would be a new man and I a new woman. What did we call his fault? Not having noticed that I no longer loved him. What was my fault? Not loving him. Which came first? This point we debated. At the end of two weeks, during which time I spoke to Pascal on the phone repeatedly, though briefly, realizing with each call that I was losing him a little more, my husband moved to a small apartment nearby. Chris shuffled cheerfully enough between us. We never argued in front of her and she didn't seem to think it unpleasant that she now possessed two residences. On the nights when she stayed with her father I lay in my bed and felt myself clutching the sheets with the disconcerting sensation of being revolved slowly in space. Was it possible that I liked being alone? The idea stunned me with pleasure and fear. I thought that I might live without Pascal or my husband. Yes, I thought, I wouldn't like it but I could do it; it was not beyond my power. Could I live without my daughter? My answer to that question was unequivocal and never faltered. No. Nor could I deny her free and constant access to her father's love. I knew she would suffer without it and that someday she would blame me for it.

I saw nothing but to divide myself more thoroughly, more publicly, than I had before among those who held a fair claim to me. This meant that I saw a great deal more of Pascal.

My life began to fill with everything stolen, and it was enormously sweet. I was forced back into full-time employment by our need to pay two rents, and so the hours I had often spent luxuriating in Pascal's company were gone, replaced now with some regularity by entire nights passed by his side. My interludes with my daughter were filled with warmth and mutual regard. Her tiny life revolved around mine. She wanted my happiness. There were times when I thought she would have fought for my happiness, so nearly did she equate it with her own. The hours I spent with my husband were often bitter, full of reproaches on both sides, rich with misunderstandings, grievances now suddenly laid bare to the light of our mutual scrutiny. They were not pleasant hours but they were necessary. I felt about going to see him as I had once felt about piano lessons: it was for my own good and someday my patience would be rewarded with unexpected freedom. I knew that he possessed what few people ever hope to possess: the ability to entirely forgive a wrong. It was only a matter of time before he would forgive me.

During the weeks that followed my separation, Pascal and I enjoyed the most purely amorous time we were ever to have. I hadn't expected him to change anything in his own life on my account but he seemed willing, even eager to do so. The spirit of cold possession that had animated him until then changed to something surprisingly warm. His physical presence ceased to be so violent. He could make of his body a wonderfully comfortable and familiar resting place or a weapon; there wasn't much in between. I began to see more of the resting place, and as I was often too tired for serious battle, I came to prefer it. It was a surprise to me that he could express as much tenderness as it became my good fortune to receive. I was slow to accept the notion that he might really care for me.

One day he announced that in a spree of house cleaning he had thrown away every useless memory he had. There stood in a corner of the room a plastic trash bag filled to its brim with crumpled papers. "It looks as if you've a lot more to forget than I do," I said.

"I'd like to forget most of my life," he said. Then he fastened the bag and gave it a soft kick.

Was this reform? I wondered. Was I having such an effect on him that he should shed a disgraceful past? Or was I, I blushed to think, only the most disgraceful woman he had met and did my antics only make the past irrevelant? My spirits were very high. I believed myself to be intensely desirable to a man I desired more than I had ever desired anyone.

It was a good thing for me to think better of Pascal, allowing me as it did to think a little better of myself. I couldn't imagine a tie with him that wouldn't make my life more difficult than it was; I certainly didn't hope for one. Instead I settled down to a concerted effort at maintaining the delicate status quo. I flattered myself that I did it well enough, which was why, when I opened my front door one day to find Claire standing uneasily on the step, I felt a small, uneasy quiver, a premonition. I had not taken my regular expedition to the Square that week, and as I looked down into her serious, urgent young face, I knew I had not done so for a reason.

She was, I saw as well in that glance, feeling awkward, hot, and tired. She had walked from Esplanade to my house, a fifteen-block walk down a shadeless sidewalk that ran between two long, unrelenting rows of house fronts, one very much like the next. She had hoped I wouldn't ask why. "I didn't know if you would be home," she said. "I hope I'm not bothering you."

I assured her that she was not, that I had just been thinking of fixing something cold to drink and sitting on my back porch, that she was welcome to join me.

We walked together through the long house and arrived, without speaking again, at the kitchen. Chris, on seeing her, came shouting in, banging the screen door, offering her the morning's greatest treasure, a bright green lizard in a bottle. "With these holes!" she cried. "So he can get air."

Claire looked at the unhappy creature through the glass while Chris and I described the joyful moment of his capture. Overhead the ceiling fan whirred sleepily and in the air the hum of insect life, which thrived in our large, shady backyard, could be heard beneath the more pleasant sound of the many birds who shared this vast, verdant paradise no more aimably than survival allowed. Claire relaxed, took her glass of ice water with a smile, felt herself welcomed, her presence a happy addition to a dull afternoon. We took chairs on the porch and looked out together at the yard, which, she explained, she would never have imagined from the street to be so lovely, so fragrant. She began to think less of why she had come; indeed, she didn't appear to know why. I thought I knew and I hoped to make her so comfortable that she would forget it entirely and go away thinking that she was now free to come and go as she pleased. As we talked of plants, of the heat, of the variety of birds, lizards, and other insect predators (in our miserable region never abundant enough), of the terrible lessons one learned from any observation of insect life, of natural topics that seemed to follow one from another, I was aware that we would make each other good friends and that such friends are rare. She had kept a garden in the convent, she and Sister Michele, an old friend, and they had conversed for hours on the most effective methods of insect control. They learned what plants to plant near one another, which bugs to pinch and which to encourage, how to recognize, by the look of the victim, the name of the enemy.

I inquired more about her friend: Did she still correspond with her?

She was distressed by my question. The past didn't come back easily to Claire, particularly when she had not, to her own mind, behaved in a perfectly satisfactory manner.

She was not supposed to have a friend, what the community called a "particular" friend, and with one exception she had not tried to have one. But she had entered the novitiate with Michele, a childhood companion whom she could not forget she knew well. They shared, besides a long family friendship, a sense of humor, a sense, they quickly perceived, missing in their fellow aspirants. Her friend had difficulty from the start and it was only a matter of weeks before Claire knew that she must take a "particular" interest if she were not to suffer a more particular loss. Michele had trouble with everything. She was late for morning prayers and sometimes fell asleep during vespers. She talked during silences, wept openly when called upon to accuse herself, and failed to make regular confessions. Sometimes as they skated around the cold, damp walls of the basement, she drew Claire aside and confided that she feared she wouldn't be able to continue. "I just don't have it," she said. "It's not that I don't want it. I want it so badly I don't have the courage to give up."

"It's supposed to be difficult," Claire replied. "That's why we're here. It's the perfect way, the ideal life. Why should it be easy?"

"I can look at you and see it's not as hard for you as it is for me," Michele said. "Does that make me better off than you?" As she said this she smiled so wanly that Claire couldn't deny her some comfort.

"I admit it," Claire replied. "I love the routine, I love having every minute filled."

"And you love the idea of having it that way forever?" her friend asked.

"Yes," she replied.

Michele nodded and skated on.

While Claire grew more contented with her vocation, she suffered to see her friend's despair. Michele had lost the good benefices of every superior she had; she had even begun to do poorly in her exams. One evening as Claire was pulling her stiff white gown over her head in preparation for sleep, there was a timid knock at the door of her cell. She opened it to find Michele, similarly gowned, with a pair of scissors in her hand. Her expression was so troubled that Claire, ignoring the rule against allowing any visitor in one's room, took her friend by the sleeve and pulled her inside. Michele seated herself quickly in the single straight-back chair and sighed deeply. "I've made up my mind," she said. "You've got to help me."

"I will if I can," Claire replied.

"You've got to cut my hair," she said, holding out the scissors.

Both girls had hair to their shoulders. They were not required to cut it and wore it, beneath their short white veils, pinned back behind their ears. Michele had loosened her thick hair now and it fell about her shoulders heavily, giving her an untamed look, despite her simple gown and slippered feet.

"Don't be ridiculous," Claire said. "How will that help you?"

"Because you're going to cut it so short I would be ashamed to show myself outside the convent."

"Michele," Claire said sadly.

"It's the only way. I know I won't leave for three months if I don't have my hair. It will take that long to grow out, and I have to give it three more months at least."

"Can't you just believe that and stay?"

Michele answered by holding the scissors up between them. "Do it quick," she said, "before someone comes."

Claire had then taken up the task, but with such reluctance that she felt every clip of the shears as if she were shredding her own conscience. She cut and cut; it took a long time. Her friend sat stiffly, not speaking, her hands pressed against her knees. Claire knew that she was weeping and was careful not to look into her face. When at last she was done she looked at the crudely shorn head and reddened eyes before her and couldn't restrain a long, pitiful sigh.

"Does it look completely dreadful?" Michele asked in a voice that registered irony as well as panic.

"Completely," Claire said. She placed the scissors in her friend's hands. Michele, giving herself a resolute shake, rose to her feet and hurried to the door. "Pray for me," she said as she went out without looking back. Claire stood looking at the closed door for a few moments. She knew, and she was sure that Michele knew too, that this last-ditch effort was doomed to failure. It puzzled her to see a spirit so divided that its will was forced to create artificial supports for itself. She fell to her knees and began gathering up the scattered locks of hair, which she then deposited in her trash can. The old janitoress would surely know what they had been up to, Claire thought, but she had a reputation for speaking only when spoken to.

Of course her friend left, having confided to Claire as

they walked back from their last tennis match that there was a boy on the outside whom she didn't dislike.

"Will you marry him?" Claire asked. She slapped her racket against the heavy folds of her brown wool skirt so that her question was punctuated with the sound of a muffled blow.

"I don't know," Michele replied. "He told me I'd never make it here. I guess he was right."

"How can you go back to someone who told you that?"

Michele smiled at her friend's ready outrage. "Because he was right," she said.

Claire thought of her friend's failure often, and the more she thought of it the more unnecessary it seemed. What was the good of having an ideal if everyone is trying to beat everyone else at admitting how impossible it is to achieve it? She recalled a lay teacher who discouraged imaginative flights with a dreary appeal to what she called "realism." "Let's be realistic," this woman implored her class several times a day. Claire hated being realistic. She believed it meant embracing personal failure, and failure was what she could not bring herself ever to embrace.

She didn't admit this that afternoon on my porch. What she didn't say, I thought, she implied. The convent life was still vivid to her; I saw it in the way she spoke with sudden irresistible surges of memory. She finished her story a little sadly, as if she regretted having spoken. She looked away, out at Chris, who was swinging on her rope swing, and she said softly, "How I look forward to going back."

"You make it sound attractive," I admitted. "Though lately I've been enjoying my freedom so thoroughly I think I would be hard put to give up a moment of it."

"Giving it up entirely is a lot easier than giving up a moment of it," she said agreeably. "If you give it up entirely it goes away entirely." She raised her hand as if to brush it away. "It ceases to be a problem."

"What a curious idea," I said. Freedom had recently come to mean something as palpable to me as my own arm, and in trying to explain this notion I told her of my separation from my husband.

"Do you mean you think of leaving your husband to have more time for Pascal?" she asked excitedly.

"I'm afraid I've done just that," I said.

"It's a mistake," she said. "You may think I'm just childish, just romantic, but I must tell you that I can see without any doubt that it's a mistake to spend any of your time with that man."

I was surprised by her frankness and tried to match it. "I don't think you romantic," I said, "but I do think you are unable to understand my feelings."

She took this in gloomy silence. As far as she was concerned she understood exactly. Then the point of diversity dawned on her and she said, as if the subject interested her, "Because I'm a virgin?"

I nodded sagely, in all my nonvirginal mystery, and I hated myself for the rush of superiority that swept through me.

"I don't see why a virgin can't tell when a man is rotten to the core," she observed. "When his conversation *alone* is always corrupting, consistently corrupting, and full of snideness and contempt for his fellows. What must something more be like!"

I laughed. "I suppose it's thoroughly corrupting," I said. "And that I am thoroughly corrupted, which is what I mean when I say you don't understand my feelings."

(126)

She sniffed to show that she still disagreed, and looked away. She had said what she had come to say, with more vehemence than she had intended, and we both knew it. Though I have entered her thoughts freely in this narrative, I confess to not having seen entirely into them at that moment. She was sworn to hate Pascal, she who had sworn to hate no one; this I could see but I wasn't sure why. I thought the strength of reaction against him disproportionate to the distaste she might rightly nourish against any man who thought her vocation a sham. She spoke as if she had dismissed him from her thoughts, but she had walked a long way to tell me that I should follow her example. I concluded that Pascal had touched on some doubt she had about herself, a sure-fire method to lay the mighty low. Pascal wouldn't be satisfied until he had proven to himself, and to Claire as well, that she was an ordinary woman. I despised him a little for this, even if he did it for the only excusable motive, that he was simply trying to find his match.

Claire continued to stare into space. "Don't you know what he wants?" she said at last, though she appeared to be putting the question to herself.

"He says he wants a reasonable world," I answered.

"What a dreadful world that would be!" she exclaimed. "Where no one is allowed to have anything but dogged, dreary little visions in which no hint of imagination or self-confidence is acceptable."

I laughed. I had the vague hope that she was indeed a match for Pascal.

EIGHTEEN

A FTER Claire went back to her mother's house, I sat
on the porch and considered my options. I knew myself to
be in an impossible position, one in which any change
would destroy my own happiness and in which change of
some kind was inevitable. Apart from the probability of
everyone's feeling much worse than they had previously,
I had one other fear. This was a force from the outside,
an uproar in society, a collective panic that might render
trivial problems like mine (whom to have sex with, whom
to love, whom to give up) not only insoluble but inappropriate. And this disturbance was fast upon us; by that time
we could feel it in the air.

A week passed and in that week there were six more
cases of the mysterious disease reported. It was curable if
caught early enough. The first symptoms were chills alternating with high fever and pains in the joints. The
difficulty seemed to be that it ran its entire course rapidly
and at the end of sixteen hours the patient was either past
help or past life itself. The six patients, three of whom
survived, all lived in one area of the city, suggesting to
some authorities that the disease could best be eliminated
by being quickly isolated. When the seventh case was re-

ported, the city health officials, who had known the disease by its proper name all along and had refrained from naming it to avoid alarming the populace, told the anxious news media the worst. It was bubonic plague, and the last case, that of a housewife from the Ninth Ward who succumbed within ten hours, was of the pneumonic variety. This meant it was no longer spread only by fleas but could now be contracted through the air, by a cough, by a kiss, by a sigh.

There was immediately talk of quarantine, but there had been as much talk of an end to the garbage workers' strike, and it was running into its twelfth week. The city government was in an uproar and had been for some time. Its main priority had been to keep the buses running and to keep the industrious citizens who attempted to dispose of their garbage by burning it in the street from burning down the city as well. The state's promise of gasoline had been revoked at the last moment and news of an epidemic in New Orleans served only to increase the chagrin of our representatives in the state capital. Only the city health officials, many of whom specialized in tropical medicine and knew as much about plague as any people in the world, recognized the gravity of the situation and tried to remedy it. One afternoon they issued a statement in which they threatened to call in a federal investigative team if some action wasn't taken immediately. And it was this threat alone that stirred our city's managers into action. Two days later I stood on my front porch and watched a long line of trucks, equipped to spray insecticide into every cranny of our neighborhood, roll down the street. They spread out and within an hour the air was acrid with poison. In the days that followed, each house was visited by a pesticide specialist, a profession that has always flourished in our city, who examined the house, sprayed chemicals on the baseboards, into closets, cabinets, piles of dirty laundry, behind appliances, beneath baby cribs, and directly onto unsuspecting dogs and cats. Three hours after my own house was inspected, my parakeet expired in his cage, but, as I pointed out to my grief-stricken daughter, he was a very old bird and there might have been no connection between the poison in our house and the death of our innocent pet.

The area outlined for quarantine was already large. It extended east to west, from the Industrial Canal to Canal Street, and north to south, from Claiborne Avenue to the river, an area of nine hundred square blocks. These borders were obvious choices, containing two natural water boundaries and two sparsely populated, essentially business areas at their outer limits. They became of interest to me, however, in this respect: Claire and I lived inside the proposed quarantine area and Pascal did not.

NINETEEN

EVERYONE tried to persuade everyone else of the proper course of action. The notion of leaving before it was too late was irresistible to a few, but mostly to those who had little to lose. Many of us thought we could best ride out an imminent disaster in the shelter of our own homes, and so we didn't seriously think of going. My husband and I discussed sending Chris to my mother, who lived well outside the designated area, but we vacillated so helplessly between the thought of her safety and the conviction that there could be no real safety for her away from us that we left it to chance. If she happened to be visiting there at the moment a quarantine was enforced, then the matter would be settled.

Claire's mother wished her to return to the safety of the convent and was quick to tell her so. But it wasn't easy to break the agreement she had made. Claire had five months to go before her prescribed year was out, and there were those, inside the cloister as well as out, who would not be provoked to change the prescription because the medicine might prove to have unexpected side effects. The mother-general at the Carmelite house wasn't eager for her to return and Father Paine wasn't willing that she should leave the city. Her own sentiments were as divided as the advice she received. She began to look for a sign from some higher authority, and one bright afternoon in September she received it.

She had just made her confession and given, she thought as she turned away from the curtain, as full and clear an account of herself as was in her power to give. It had cost her a lot and she stood for a moment, her shoulders slouched forward, her head inclined a little back, her arms relaxed at her sides, as if, had she only the energy, she would lift her arms and fly away. Her heart ached. She fancied she could have pointed out the place where the pain was if someone were to hold that heart out before her. Father Paine had suggested that, while he never doubted her sincerity, he sometimes feared that she didn't possess a generous heart. This idea had struck her as boldly as if she had just seen herself described in a textbook. She couldn't conceive of a person more sinful than herself. Her resolutions, she thought, were as useless to her Lover as the dust. He had made her to be something she hadn't the courage to be; He had made her to engage her heart, but she withheld her heart.

She stood in the nave in a delirium of despair. She was afraid to pray. Her Lover would see through the prayer; she knew it. He would see how she sought to please Him by continually avoiding the one thing He asked of her. She could give Him a lifetime on her knees, and at the end she would be no more than she was at the moment, a creature who was afraid to be where He had placed her.

She heard Father Paine's step behind her and she turned toward him, her hands held out as if to push him away.

"I think we should talk about it a little more," he said, indicating the back of the church. "As a friend, not as your confessor."

"What more can you say?" she replied. "You're exactly right about me and we both know it."

"If only it were that simple," he said. "That would make my job an easy one."

"What should I do?" she said impatiently. "I think you know and you won't tell me."

"Let's go in the kitchen," he said. "I guess I can tell you what I think you shouldn't do."

She followed him gloomily through the church and out into the narrow shade-filled alley that separated the church from the rectory. As they passed the garden she looked in at the statue of her Lord. Then Father Paine ushered her through the door, along the narrow hall, and into the bright kitchen. The church supplied him with a maid, and his house, so little inhabited, was always meticulously clean. That day a fresh bowl of azaleas had been placed on the kitchen table and the black-and-white-tiled floor had received a coat of wax. The room sparkled, but as its furnishings were all old and worn, its brightness comforted the eye. Claire slipped into a chair and sat quietly while the priest filled two glasses with water. Then he sat across from her, just far enough away so that he couldn't reach her with his hand outstretched.

Claire drank from her glass and cleared her throat. But before she could speak, he asked, "Why do you seek the contemplative life?"

"I have a vocation for it. I was made for it. I could never be happy with any other life."

"What is it about it that appeals to you?"

"The routine, the opportunity for being . . ." She paused, waiting for the right word. "Collected," she concluded.

"And the safety?" the priest suggested.

"I'm tired of hearing that," she snapped. "Why is it

running away to embrace a life in which perfection is the goal?"

"Because you're surrounded by others who recognize your goal, who will help you on with it if they can."

She looked up. "I see all other people as potential occasions of sin," she said. "That's my problem. I'm constantly wary. I can't trust anyone."

"Do you trust me?"

She hid her face in her hands. "I don't know," she whispered.

"Then you've taken this thing too far."

"I know," she said.

"What do you fear from me?"

She replied at once. "That you might love me."

The priest smiled drily. "I've spent my life being wary too," he said. "I imagine I could outdo you at that any day."

"You're wary of me?" Claire asked. Her eyes widened at this new idea.

"What I fear for you is that someday you may be as unable to love as I am. I don't want you to end up like me."

"I can't think of anyone I'd rather resemble."

"I know it," he said. "I appreciate it. But I'm telling you that you have the strength I never had and you can do better."

"And what could be better?"

The priest was silent.

"Being a wife?" she said contemptuously. "Being a mother? Being a banker, a political woman?"

Still he didn't speak.

"My options are limited, Father," she said. "I'm a woman."

"And you want to be a saint," he said.

This time it was she who remained quiet. He watched a smile quivering about her lips and for the first time in the conversation their eyes met and held. Claire's little smile became larger. "Yes," she said, nodding and smiling through a vision that threatened to blur with tears. "Oh, yes."

Father Paine smiled too, though not so joyfully as his penitent. He felt a little stab of pain in his head. He was about to counsel her to stay near him and all at once he wasn't certain (though he had convinced himself that he was certain) of advising her with only her best interest in mind. He looked down. "Well, you may be yet," he said quickly. "And I hope for it. And I hope it will be in spite of me."

Claire stopped smiling as suddenly as she had started. "I want you to decide this problem for me," she said. "I'm under no binding orders anywhere and I want to be in the place where I'll be of most use to the Church. Shall I go back, or shall I stay?"

"Most people believe," he said, "that this quarantine, should it be imposed, will be over in a matter of weeks."

"I've heard that," she said.

"If this is true, then you should keep your promise and return to Lacombe only when you've completed the time you agreed upon."

"Of course," she said softly.

"If this epidemic is brought under control quickly, it will cost you nothing," he continued. "And if it isn't, there will be work for you here."

"I guess I should pray to Saint Roch then," she said with a laugh.

The priest shrugged. "It couldn't hurt."

Claire pushed her chair back and preceded him through the door. In the alley she turned to him. "Thank you," she said. "I came here thinking my way was clear and now I'm perfectly muddled. I'll do as you say, though I never thought I would."

"Any time," he said, turning back toward the house. "Call me when you need me."

They were so like lovers parting, contented with each other and at peace with the world they would now look on apart, that they couldn't fail to notice it. The priest closed the door quickly and Claire turned to look down the alley. She had been gloomy and hopeless; now she found herself lighthearted. She smiled at two children who ran by her and she strolled in a leisurely way back into the church. She chose a pew in the rear and sat back in it so that her face was in shadow. The sweetness of the natural world filled her senses. She thought of the smallness of it, the vastness of it, the wonderful science of it. To think of nature and see herself in it gave her a kind of two-way vision, so that she felt the eyes of her soul magnifying the heavens like the lenses of a telescope. To fear an inner life, she thought, was the greatest foolishness. It was like fearing a breath of air. Why did people find it harder to admit to a universe within than without? Why trust, for a moment, one's own absurd measurement of either?

TWENTY

——

I TOO was given to an awe of nature, but the wonder that confounded me was the human body, in particular Pascal's body as he used it to disassemble my senses in his small apartment.

One evening as we lay face to face, side by side, my legs wrapped around his back, comfortably, companionably, I reflected that I was relaxed for the first time in days. He began to move against me and when I raised myself on one elbow I found myself looking down at the knife, which lay open on the bed. I had noticed it earlier. Pascal saw me glance and reached back for it, feeling gingerly about for the handle. Then, smiling, he placed it against my throat. "Don't make a false move," he said.

"No," I replied, smiling back, "I won't." He held the blade there, careful not to press the edge against my skin, for several moments. I had no fear of his cutting me, even though he moved against me more and more rapidly and was clearly excited. His face was flushed, his eyes closed, and in a show of unconscious concern, he took the knife away. He meant, I think, to put it on the table but as he reached across me the blade caught my shoulder. His eyes opened and he drew in a quick breath, freezing midthrust

(137)

in an expression of surprise, even, I thought, of horror. But though I could feel the blood collecting in the hollow below my clavicle, I had scarcely felt the cut, it was so quick and I had been so excited at the moment.

"Jesus, I'm sorry," Pascal whispered. He had dropped the knife alongside the bed and now I saw that he expected me to be angry and that he genuinely regretted the accident.

"Don't worry about it," I said. "Don't stop."

"Really?" I had taken his hips in my hands and sought to pull him back down. "But you're bleeding."

I knew I was bleeding and that it would soon run off onto the sheets, but I was also on the edge of a cataclysmic orgasm that seemed, at that moment, more important. "Put your mouth over it," I said. "Please."

Then he saw my dilemma and gave in to it. He pressed his mouth against my shoulder, licking the blood away and arriving at his climax in the trembling conclusion of my own. He began to suck at the small wound, hesitant and anxious. Nor did I feel any pain from it, for I was delirious with pleasure.

Later, when I sat on my own couch alone, I wept with the memory of it. In the midst of his embraces I found I sometimes longed for death; I felt I was ready to go beyond the limitations of my senses if only I could take him with me. There is something to be said for a lover with whom one can be united *only* in death. I thought of Claire's determination to have her spiritual Lover when I saw Pascal's face looking down at me. His expressions were always agreeable, interested, friendly, even jovial when we began, but by the time he arrived at his nerve-shattering orgasm, he looked as if he would dearly like to kill me. It crossed my mind that eventually he would.

After a time I came to realize that I had never loved anyone as I loved him, that most people never experience such a passion, that I had been incredibly, divinely fortunate to have found, in a world where most souls dig their own graves with the sharp edge of their bitter loneliness, my true, my beloved mate.

But I was not his, I was not my husband's, I was not my own. My whole manner had become one of alternating fits of submission and assertive independence.

One day when I was submissive Pascal brought up the question of the quarantine. "You'll be right in the middle of it," he said. "Don't you think you should move out?"

I gave my rote reply. "I can't leave my house," I said. "It would be burned. All the money I have is tied up in that house."

"So what?" he said. "If you get this disease you'll be dead."

"Not necessarily. And the quarantine area is huge," I said. "It's really arbitrary. You could get it as easily as I."

He gave me a long, serious look. "You could stay here," he said.

"I can't leave my daughter."

"Then bring her with you."

I laughed.

"I don't see what's funny about it."

"No," I said. "It's just that it's impossible. It's very kind of you, but it's just not possible."

He looked down at his own knees and I knew that I had hurt him. I thought that one thing that would make it impossible for me to live with him was that I wouldn't want Chris to hear even a whisper of what went on between us. He saw this and resented it.

"But thank you," I said.

"I won't be able to see you," he said.

That was when I first understood what we faced. There would be a street between Pascal and me, and we would not, either of us, be allowed to cross it.

"It won't last long," I said. "And you could always come in, I guess."

"I suppose that will get harder the longer it lasts," he said.

We were silent. I lay at his side thinking of it, but I couldn't picture a life without him. If I had, I might not have left him that day.

For during that night, while most of the city was asleep, a long row of army trucks made a quiet procession down the highway from Baton Rouge. When they arrived in New Orleans they fanned out along a preordained route. Many of the trucks contained groups of National Guardsmen, huddled together with their rifles across their knees. Some contained metal sawhorses, such as are used to make barricades for impassable streets. These they set out along Canal Street, from Claiborne to the river, and along Claiborne Avenue, in a huge curve to the Industrial Canal, and finally on Poland Street, along the canal to the river. When I got up the next morning and looked out into the hot September sun, my first thought was that summer was lingering, as usual, too long. It was Sunday; they had planned that so as to minimize the hysteria of workers who would not be able to get to their jobs. I didn't learn that we could no longer travel freely in our city until ten o'clock, when my husband phoned me. He had read the news in the morning paper.

TWENTY-ONE

D URING the first weeks we were turned entirely in upon ourselves and we found the psychological distance between neighbors cut in half. We still had our radios, the phones worked, and news from the outside was easily had, but the fact that it had become the "outside," that events on our streets were reported as having occurred inside the quarantine, this made us all insanely suspicious and we believed nothing if it was not gossip. That the frequency of the disease increased dramatically once we were closed off only made us more resentful. We had been sealed in, we thought, to die.

Those who contracted the disease had to report to the hospital early in the course of their illness; a few hours, we quickly learned, made the difference. Mothers panicked, rushing into the emergency room with children who had mild sore throats, headaches, or, in the case of babies too young to speak, bad dispositions.

We found ourselves with no central organizing agency we could trust. Some obligations fell naturally on the churches. Priests who had administered no greater comfort than the confessional now spent their nights consoling distraught parishioners. Many of these believed they were about to come into direct contact with the will of an un-sympathetic God and they turned on his commissioners with a vengeance. Father Paine often worked all night in the hospital emergency ward. Later, when people began to distrust the medical profession, he went from house to house. It was impossible to convince some families of those who were truly afflicted with the disease that time was of the essence. They thought only to keep their sick to themselves. Others wanted to turn from the house anyone who didn't own to feeling in extraordinarily good health, in the hope of preserving the rest of their families.

The death tolls were now reported weekly, and though they were not astounding — fifteen one week, seventeen the next, twelve the next — they did not, as had been promised, recede entirely. The disease couldn't quite get the necessary stronghold on our population to begin its mathematical progression, nor were we sufficiently vigilant to wipe it out altogether. What we felt more strongly than the dread of disease was the difficulty of provisioning ourselves and, for all those like myself who were employed beyond the quarantine boundaries, the possibility of running entirely out of money.

Claire was everywhere and always occupied. Not hampered with a clear memory of a time when things ran smoothly, she took things as she found them. She was good at organizing people and good at comforting those she couldn't organize. When residents of the French Quarter began endangering their lives by burning their garbage in their narrow streets, she was instrumental in clearing certain areas, including the yard behind the Cathedral, for the purpose. She headed a church committee that managed the distribution of food. She spent her evenings at the hospital with Father Paine or in homes where parents wept over the fate of their children and cursed her intrusion.

Sometimes I was with her. I worked because there was so much work, as well as for the small pay we received from various Church funds. Some mornings I was up at dawn and out on the streets, where the air was charged with futility and determination, the way it must be, I imagined, in a city under siege. Chris walked with me or I carried her on my back. She stood in lines for food, stood behind counters while I gave out food, sat on the floor at neighborhood meetings, clutching her teddy bear, or on the ground at dusk, watching the street fires light up. She didn't accompany me to the hospital; on those days she stayed with her father. I went there with Father Paine and Claire two days a week and what I observed was the great wonder of modern medicine, the sterilization of everything, of ugliness, of pain, of death itself. Many people contracted the disease and recovered. This was what kept our streets quiet at night.

One night Claire and I sat in the long, poorly lit hall of the emergency ward, consoling the mother of a child. She had brought in her little girl, having walked two miles with the child screaming in her arms. What we all knew as we sat there, waiting to hear the fate of this child, was that the mother had been enormously, almost homicidally stupid. Everyone knew the symptoms of plague by now, and the child, from the mother's babbled, tearful account, had exhibited them clearly. When her armpits had begun to swell, the mother had given her a warm bath, then placed ice packs against the swellings in the insane hope of bringing them down. On examining the child, the doctor on duty, after asking serious, patient questions, had suddenly turned on the woman and accused her of being an idiot. "Why didn't you call an ambulance? Why didn't you call a neighbor?" he shouted.

"I didn't know," she stuttered. "I thought it was something else."

The child, surrounded by nurses and already so sedated that the pain she was in filled her face only with a hazy, worried interest, called out, "Mama, stay with me." But they were already wheeling her down the hall, and the mother, who knew her negligence wouldn't be tolerated one step deeper into the sacrosanct, sterile womb of the hospital, sank into a chair and hid her face in her hands.

I looked at her with a feeling compounded of wonder, horror, and sympathy. It was not the Middle Ages, I thought. Our entire population wasn't threatened. The disease was often enough not even fatal. But surely the death counts, which now appeared daily on the front page of the newspaper, the shortages of food, of services, the street fires, the closed schools, the strained, nervous faces of our citizens, the fact, more noticeable every day, that we lived inside a quarantine, surely these things should cause a certain overcautiousness in the detection of a child's illness. Many of us rationalized our hysteria bravely every day. My own concession to it had been to have my daughter sleep with me, so that when I woke in the night overpowered by the fear of losing her, I could take her in my arms, feel her cool forehead, breathe her innocent breath, and assure myself that she was still well, still my own.

How could this woman have been so poorly prepared? How could she have refused to see that the cruel hand we all feared had come to rest on the head of her own child? A wave of revulsion overcame me and I looked away. Claire went to the woman and knelt before her. "Do you have any other children?" she asked.

The woman looked down at her, unable to speak. She nodded her head.

"How many?" Claire asked.

"Three," she said with an effort. "I left them home."

"You've done all you can do for this one. You should go back to the others."

The woman sat up straight, straining to look down the hall where her daughter had disappeared.

"My little girl," she said. "I can't leave her. She's my baby."

"There's nothing you can do here," Claire said. "If you leave your phone number with me, I'll call you as soon as we find out anything."

The woman looked quizzically into Claire's face. She didn't appear to understand what she heard but to have alighted on some other plan than the one Claire proposed. "Who are you?" she said.

Claire glanced back at me, a hurried, nervous look that told me she didn't want to answer this question. "My name is Claire," she said.

The woman's eyes opened wide. "You're Sister Claire D'Anjou, aren't you?" she said.

"I was," Claire replied. "But I've left the order."

"You saved Lottie Pratt's girl!" the woman exclaimed. She took Claire's hands in her own. "She told me all about it. The doctors said her girl would die, but then you prayed over her and she didn't die."

"I pray for all the children here," Claire replied. "Some die, some don't."

"No!" the woman cried, standing up. "You can save my

little girl." She directed Claire toward the hall. "Go down there and pray over her now. Go and touch her. Her name is Jane, Jane Leary. I know you can do it."

Claire pulled away from the woman, protesting mildly. "I can't save anyone. I will pray for your child, but I don't even pray that lives be spared. I pray that God will take all children to His heart, as He promised."

"I don't care what you say," the woman replied. "You go and pray over my girl now. I know you can save her when those doctors can't. I know you can."

Claire turned to me. "Emma," she said, "would you show Mrs. Leary how to get out while I go see about her daughter?"

I realized I had been watching this scene with the unarticulated hope of being left out of it. I took Mrs. Leary's arm from Claire and began leading her back to the reception area. "She's a saint," Mrs. Leary confided to me. "She can save my Jane."

My patience was worn thin and I gave Mrs. Leary unsolicited advice as I pulled her toward the exit doors. "Go home," I said. "See to your other children. And watch them carefully all night. If any of them have headaches or fever, or if they say their legs and arms are sore, call an ambulance and send them here at once. Do you understand?"

"Yes," she said. "I'll go. Now I know Jane will be all right."

"Watch the children you have left," I said coldly, propelling her to the glass doors, which flew open before us. I watched her as she went along the sidewalk, mumbling to herself, calling on the powers of superstition, which, above all else, she trusted. When I returned to the reception hall I found Claire waiting for me. If she had prayed over Mrs. Leary's child, she hadn't formed more than three words. When I joined her she lifted her chin, indicating the street and the confused soul we had turned out upon it. "What a disagreeable woman," she said.

"I didn't know you were a saint," I said.

Claire looked away and it struck me that the idea, though perplexing, was not, as I had imagined, a joke to her. "She's afraid," she said.

"She should have thought of that earlier," I said, turning away.

In a few hours one of the interns informed us that Mrs. Leary's daughter was dead. Claire requested the unhappy task of informing the mother. I never knew what words passed between them.

Claire and I worked together often when we were in the hospital and we came to depend on each other for the detachment we needed, as we had on the day we saw the dying rats. I sometimes thought that scene itself had designated us as insiders. I found the suffering of the children hard to bear, but I was otherwise satisfied with my place in what had become a heartless machinery for survival.

Sometimes I walked to Canal Street and looked at the barricades. The Guardsmen had grown tired of their work after the first week and they watched those of us who came to watch them with weary vigilance. No cases of the disease had been reported outside the quarantine area; the rest of the city went on freely, as if some rotten part of it had been cut out with a paring knife. There were individual struggles with the terms given us. Divided families sought to be reunited. But there was no organized resistance to the quarantine, and so it went on, week after week, while the death tolls rose and fell and rose again.

TWENTY-TWO

A FEW weeks later, Pascal found himself on Claiborne and Canal, the corner where big trucks came and unloaded their supplies into smaller trucks maintained inside the quarantine. The government gasoline supplies were so erratic that sometimes our trucks were drawn by horses. On this day, however, we were well supplied and the scene before him gave no hint of the privation we occasionally endured. He watched some men carrying great boxes of fresh vegetables from one spot to another. He noticed a woman, hard at work, and he looked at her back admiringly for some moments without recognizing her.

She was lifting boxes of canned food from the lower step of a truck and transferring them to a wheelbarrow. She had lost twelve pounds since the last time he had seen her, and her arms, as they moved from left to right, looked pathetically weak. When the wheelbarrow was full she brushed her forehead with the back of her forearm and turned to face him.

She had been, he saw at once, transformed. Though her body was smaller, thinner, paler, she appeared, paradoxically, to have taken on strength. Her eyes didn't burn with religious fervor as they once had. They were, as she surveyed the dull scene before her, perfectly lucid, serene, as detached from the realm of feeling as the eyes of a woman who had been beaten senseless. Her face had taken on angularity. He didn't remember her nose as being so pronounced, and there were two hectic spots of color at her cheekbones that couldn't be mistaken for the blush of health. She recognized Pascal at last and smiled briefly across the barrier before she turned back to her work, for the wheelbarrow had been emptied and was ready to be reloaded.

He couldn't move. Desire flooded his every cell with such force that he felt his knees weakening, his heart quickening, the pores of his body opening as if to expel excessive fluid. He took in the delicate curve of her neck, the slightly pendulous movement of her breasts as she lifted another box and swung it across her thighs so that it landed with a thump in the wheelbarrow. He took in her legs, which were planted firmly apart, and through her dark skirt he thought he could detect the fragile swivel of the hipbones in their sockets. A man came up to her, spoke to her, relieved her, and without looking back at Pascal, she walked off in the direction of the Square. Pascal called her name, once, in a voice that struck him as unnaturally hoarse and dry and that, evidently, didn't carry across the crowded street, for Claire continued to move away without looking back.

He didn't hesitate. In a moment he had spoken to the guard, and the metal horse was being dragged aside. The rules were simple: anyone could enter, no one could leave. He crossed the loading zone quickly and walked up Conti Street, straining his eyes to make out her dark, small figure as she moved noiselessly toward the Square.

He caught up with her on the steps of the Cathedral.

When he called out her name this time she turned to him, clearly surprised to see him, and came back down the few steps she had crossed.

"Pascal," she said, "what are you doing here?"

"I've come in," he said breathlessly. "Just now."

She considered this a moment. "Did Emma know you were coming?"

"No. Of course not. I just decided, just now."

"You'd better call her," she said, turning away.

Pascal grasped her by the elbow and pulled her toward him. "Wait," he said.

"What are you doing?" she replied, pulling herself free as she spoke.

"I've already done it," he said. "I saw you and I followed you."

"What do you want from me?" Claire asked icily. She was annoyed with him but it dawned on her that he had thrown most of his good sense to the wind and crossed into the quarantine area on her account.

Pascal calmed himself. He couldn't, for a moment, comprehend his own urgency. "I find . . ." he said, looking about nervously. He stepped closer and touched her cheek with his palm. "I do care for you," he concluded. "I wanted to tell you that."

"I can't do anything about that," she said.

He looked down. "You haven't thought about it," he said. "If you would . . ."

"You could make me care?" she finished his sentence for him.

"Yes," he replied.

"That's impossible."

"I don't see why," he said.

"I'm sorry," she answered. "I can see that what you're

feeling has overpowered you and you think it must overpower me too. But it's nothing to me, Pascal. I don't value what you're feeling. I can't value it."

"I assure you," Pascal insisted, "it's valuable."

"I've already been overpowered," Claire explained. "And I didn't get that way by thinking about whether or not to turn down the kind of offer you make me. I had to turn that down first to get where I am, turn down any possibility of it ever for me."

As she spoke Pascal watched her face. His sense of urgency had faded a little and he felt himself in the uncomfortable position of pressing a suit he had lost faith in. Her words had no effect on him. He took her arm again and led her up the stairs to the church, for the sun was blinding them both. "You look dreadful," he said. "What have you been doing to yourself? Do you weigh a hundred pounds? It's a crime not to take better care of yourself."

She endured his fussing and when they were inside tried another tack. "I know you see everything I do as a perversity on my part," she said. He nodded his agreement. "You think I'm too devoted to an idea to see the real world, but it's through this idea that I see the world and I see it more clearly than you. It gives me perfect vision. I'm not deceived by the landscape, and not by human love. I can see it exactly as it is."

"And what is it?" he said, pushing her up against the cool stone wall. They stood before a statue of St. Thérèse of Lisieux; she held her sprig of roses out over a rack of burning candles, waiting for those converts she had promised herself.

"Human love," Claire said coldly, "is hell. I want nothing to do with it."

Pascal stepped back. Her face as she stared at him was

pale and drawn and she looked like a statue herself. He had touched her three times in this brief interview and each time he had been stunned by the coldness of her skin. Her eyes, however, seemed capable of setting flame to the object of their scrutiny and it was this that made him, at last, turn away from her without speaking. He crossed the narthex and looked back. "Did you hear what you just said?" he called to her. Then he went out into the bright light of the street.

He knew nothing of the uncontrollable quivering that overtook Claire as she stood against the wall where he had left her. Her own words rang in her head. She hated herself for having said them and she regretted them, but there they were, again and again, like the grim tolling of a bell that announces, to all who will listen, the hopeless going forth of another human soul.

Father Paine came out of the church as she stood there, and found her, her hands spread over her eyes and her face averted. He went to her at once, saying her name softly. She lifted her eyes to his, then covered them again.

"What is it?" he said. "What's happened? Has someone hurt you?"

She made an effort at self-control, rubbing her eyes with the knuckles of her hands. "No," she said. "I've just been stupid and I'm angry with myself."

"What did you do?" he said.

"It's nothing. A friend of Emma's. Pascal. It was something he said."

"Do you know him very well?" he asked.

"No," she said. She shuddered, looking so forlorn that he pitied her.

"You're working so hard," he said. "You need some rest.

Go home and get in bed and tell your mother I'll call in the morning."

"But Emma and I have to go work at the food center," she protested.

"Don't worry about it. I'll stay here and when she comes I'll go with her. I'm free for the rest of the day."

"All right," she said.

"And rest," he added. "And don't worry about anything."

She nodded and went away. I saw her walking past the Presbytère toward Chartres when I came out across the Square. I called to her but she didn't hear me. Then I saw Father Paine standing on the steps. He stood very still without looking away from Claire's retreating back until I had joined him on the stairs.

"Is something wrong?" I asked.

He smiled his sad smile. He was physically a very plain man and he gave the impression of wishing not to offend anyone by asking them to look at him. "I've sent her home. She's overtired and it seems a friend of yours has upset her," he said.

"A friend of mine?" I asked. "Who?"

"A man named Pascal."

"That's impossible," I said. "Pascal lives outside."

"Nevertheless," he said, "he was here."

I was startled. I had spoken to Pascal on the phone the day before and as usual we had bemoaned our separation. Why would he have come in to harass Claire, and why hadn't I known about it?

"So she's gone to bed," Father Paine continued. "And I'll take her place at the food center. You'll have to show me how to do what you do."

"We unpack boxes," I said. "There's nothing to it." I

led the way back to Decatur Street, Father Paine shuffling along quietly at my side. We had gone nearly two blocks before I realized that I had imposed a shocked silence between us at the mention of Pascal's name. Father Paine did not and would not intrude into my reasons for it. I decided to choose a safer topic.

"Do you think Claire is ill?" I asked.

He gave me a sidelong look in which he told me that he didn't think she was coming down with the plague. "She's too thin," he said. "She works herself too hard. She doesn't seem to be able to relax."

He seemed willing to speak of her candidly and so I asked him a question I had long wanted to ask. "Do you think she's hysterical?" I asked.

"No," he replied at once, "I don't. And I should know. I've made myself interested in every kind of hysteria you can think of. I've had to. And there's been only one person I could say this about with any surety. She doesn't appear to me to be the least hysterical."

"Do you think she's being singled out?" I said. "By someone divine?"

"No, I don't think that," he said. "I never have been able to imagine a God who chooses some souls for His service and ignores the rest. In fact I can't think of God very well at all. I mean of Divine Love. I don't understand how that would be. I accept all that on faith, of course." He paused, giving me a long look. He wanted to explain his position regarding Claire, I could see that; it was as if he knew he would be called on to do it again and again. "But I do believe in evil," he continued. "I think there are forces, sometimes embodied in people, that operate for ill, for the universal ill. Does that seem absurd to you?"

"I've thought as much myself from time to time," I said. "I never can decide."

"Well, I think it's true and you don't have to go far to find examples to support such an idea."

"I know *that's* true," I said.

"I also think that virtue can be embodied, but that it's rare. That's how I think of Christ."

"And Claire?" I added.

"I don't see any evil in her," he admitted, wondering aloud. "She can be very alarming, very determined. She will do whatever she wants, and she wants to do something extraordinary."

"You sound as if you expect her to move on," I observed. We had arrived at the glass doors of the food center and as I made this last remark he looked up and came upon his own reflection. "Do you know how many confessions I've heard?" he wailed. "Do you know what all those confessions are like?"

I sighed. "I'm not a Catholic," I said.

He turned his attention to me. "You're not? I assumed you were."

"No," I said. "So I don't even know what my own confession would be like."

"Well, you'll have to take my word for it," he said. "Claire's confessions are different. They are" — he paused — "real engagements with the will."

Then, as he pulled the door open for me and I passed through, he added, "And she shames me."

TWENTY-THREE

WHEN I opened my front door that night the phone was ringing. I knew it was Pascal and didn't hurry to answer it. I had worked all day with the thought of what I wanted to say to him, and I doubted that I possessed the courage to follow through with any of it. It would be, I thought, a riot of information, his trying to tell me where he was and why and my trying to tell him that I knew he was lying.

"Emma," he said, "I've done something surprising." He sounded so cheerful, so confident that I would be pleased that I was tempted to let the lie pass.

"You've come inside the quarantine," I said flatly.

"Yes." He was hesitant. "How did you know?"

"Because I've seen Father Paine, who has seen Claire, who has seen you."

He paused. "News travels fast," he said.

"Where are you staying?" I asked.

He named his hotel. "It's like another country here," he said. "Like a ghetto."

"You were an idiot to do it," I said. I felt suddenly furious with him and at the same time anxious to see him. It had been so long, I thought. I had spoken to him every day,

(156)

but now, here, unbidden, was the possibility of touching him again. "Why did you do it?"

"It can't last much longer," he said. "I told you I'd have some time off soon and I wanted to see you. I wish you'd come over here right now. Or can I come to you?"

Settle it face to face, I thought. "No, I'll come there," I said. "I'm on my way."

After we hung up I called my husband and told him there was some emergency I had to attend to. I had told him this truthfully often enough for him to think it credible. He agreed to keep Chris and cautioned me against walking alone. Then I bathed, dressed hurriedly, and went out into the street. Pascal's hotel was thirty blocks from my house, a distance, I judged, I could travel easily on my bike. As I rode through the dark streets I had the eerie sensation of giving off light and of being perfectly isolated. The streets were empty; people no longer sat on their steps at night for fear of breathing in their death. My way passed the doorway of Claire's house and I thought of her in her room, struggling with her young soul.

And then I thought of my own soul, which, like my body, had healed a little since the quarantine began. I wasn't ashamed of the way I spent my days. My relations with my fellows were amicable. I consoled myself with my daughter, and that consolation, I had to admit, was considerable. But my life was sexless, frustration was my most powerful emotion, and I had nearly forgotten what it was like to lie as still and as satisfied as Pascal had so often left me.

Satisfied? I thought. Or just exhausted, drained, as good as dead.

I didn't want to see him again, to start it again. I would tell him that and leave.

In a few minutes I was locking my bike up at the hotel door. Pascal, who had been standing in the lobby, came out to meet me. He looked thinner, paler, but that observation was lost in the general alarm the sight of him caused me. I felt my resolutions dissolve within me. The long nights I had spent holding my daughter, my eyes following the track of the moonlight across the walls, sleepless, remembering his mouth, his eyes, his voice, the days in the hospital, prying information from the families of the sick, arranging the special quarantines of certain houses, typing requests for the movement of the dead from holding morgues to funeral homes, calling strangers, hour after hour — "your husband is dead; your wife is dead; your child is dead" — the endless, boring meetings, the long walks back home through empty streets, where the air was strange and thick with the smoke of the street fires, the weariness and loneliness of my days and nights, all these overpowered me as my lover approached, and when he reached me I fell into his arms with gratitude. He was still alive, he was still my strong, dear love, and apart from him there was only bitterness, hopelessness, a world in which desire was an embarrassment and passion a thing unknown.

He held me for a moment and I felt his lips against my skull and my neck. "Emma," he said. "Darling. Let's go in." He led me into the hotel, through the long hall, and into the elevator.

In the room I looked around. As I had suspected, there was no luggage. "Didn't you bring anything with you?" I asked.

"No. Just the clothes on my back. I've been planning

(158)

this for a while, but when the time came it was an impulse."

This annoyed me; he must think me stupid. "I thought as much," I said. "But it wasn't an impulse to see me."

"Who else?" he said, as if the idea amused him.

"Claire."

"Don't be ridiculous. I ran into her this morning, at the Cathedral. It was an accident."

"I think you came in to see her," I said.

"Why would I want to see her? And anyway, I've seen her and she's as silly as ever."

"I want you to leave her alone."

"Gladly," he said. "And perhaps I should leave you alone too."

"That might be wise."

He gave me a horrified look. "What have I done? I've come into this" — he gestured widely, including the world at large — "pest hole for you and you tell me it may not be wise to see you? I'm here for you, Emma. Not for Claire. You're a fool if you don't know it."

I began to cry and I turned away so that he wouldn't see it. "What do you want with her?"

"God knows. You think you know. You tell me."

"She's very fine," I said. "I couldn't bear to see her ruined."

"And am I ruin? Are you ruined by me?"

"Yes," I said.

"Oh, Christ!" he cried. "Why did I come here?"

"We both know that," I said.

He was quiet for a moment. Then, as if he had just heard the conversation a second time, he asked, "Do you really think you've been ruined by me?"

"Yes," I said coldly.

He smiled.

"What's funny about that?" I asked.

"I thought it was the other way around."

I considered this. "Don't be an ass," I replied. "How could it be?"

Now he stood near me and in despair I sat down on the bed and put my head in my hands. Pascal sat down beside me and put his arm around me. "How could that be?" I said again, more to myself than to him.

"I know it has to be you who caused"— he paused, wrapping his hand through my hair — "this." I didn't look up but studied my palms intently. "Because I've never been involved in anything like it before. Or since."

"Do you think I have?" I asked.

"Emma," he said softly. He pressed his mouth against the nape of my neck, holding me immobile by pulling my hair forward. I felt his tongue, sharp and wet against my ear. He took my earlobe between his teeth and bit it, gently at first, then harder. At the same time he slipped his hand beneath my blouse and closed it over my breast. His hand was cold and I started forward, but he held me fast. My chin was pressed into my breastbone and I found myself gazing at my hands, which were loosely folded in my lap. "Pascal," I said. Still holding me firmly, he lifted himself from the bed, swinging one leg around my back so that I sat, when he had readjusted me, between his legs, my back to him, my head still pressed forward. He held my hair so tightly that it hurt and I tried to lift my head to relieve the pain. Then he released me and I fell back against him, turning my head and shoulders toward him, eager for his mouth against my own. But he stopped me, held my chin in his hand for a moment, gazing at me with that look of consternation and desire that I recognized, that I had longed for, and that I understood, for the first time, I caused.

But I buried that thought and many others in the long embrace that followed. The pleasure of being touched, and not tentatively, of being pressed, pulled, squeezed breathless, of having my legs parted roughly, eagerly, of having my blouse pulled away impatiently, these pleasures banished all desires save one, the desire for more. Yet there was something different, something, I knew as I lifted my hips so that he might pull away my jeans, wrong. I was breathless and I knew it; my eyes had glazed over with desire and I knew it. It was as if I had moved outside myself, and what I saw worried me. You're done for, my friend, I thought. And you've done it to yourself.

Pascal had pulled my arms behind me, holding them at the elbows with one hand while with the other he pressed me forward. He sighed, caressing my back with his tongue; then, abruptly, he released my arms and pushed me forward so that I fell on my hands and knees to the floor.

"What do you want me to do?" he asked.

"I don't know," I said. "Everything."

"Stay like that for a minute."

I didn't move. I looked down at the carpet that stretched between my hands. It was green and it looked new. Who could afford to carpet a hotel in times like these? I thought. I could hear Pascal behind me, taking off his clothes. I heard the metallic clink as his belt buckle hit the bed. Why don't you move? I asked myself. Are you afraid?

Outside, the rain that had threatened all day burst through at last. The sweeping, heavy sound of it penetrated even into this chamber, and even my preoccupied consciousness heard it, noted it. I lifted my head toward the window.

"How nice," Pascal said, and the sound of his voice told

me that he was kneeling just behind me. His hands caressed my thighs. I felt again his lips and tongue against my lower back, moving confidently down. I shivered. Did he mean how nice that it was raining or how nice to see me on my knees again? Then I wondered at myself. The rain drummed on outside the window and on the wide stones of the hotel patio, heavy, with a sweet insistence, the kind of rain that brings cooler air with it, that is, in tropical climates, welcomed by everyone whether it inconveniences them or not. It was falling, I imagined, in my yard, beating down the big plantain trees, ripping their leaves so that they looked like tattered flags in the wind, and it was beating a few blocks away, at my husband's house, where my daughter might hear it, sitting up in her bed, thinking of me.

I sat up. Pascal turned me so that I faced him on my knees. He kissed me and I opened my mouth and arms willingly, but still I thought of the rain and how it was falling over the city. I imagined thousands of faces looking out of windows, all with the common intention of observing the rain. Pascal forced me backward until I lay sprawled on the rug. He pulled my legs wide apart and pressed himself into me, holding my arms out at my sides as he had done that first time, so long ago. The rug hurt my back and I tried to raise myself a little, but he held me down. At first I thought I would bear it, but gradually I became aware of how much it hurt and I struggled again. Pascal held me down. I felt his teeth sinking into my shoulder.

"Please," I said. "You're hurting me."

For reply he moaned softly, released my arms, and pulled my legs up roughly until my knees nearly touched the carpet behind my shoulders.

This relieved my back but hurt my legs. I couldn't understand what was wrong with me, for though I was often aching after leaving Pascal, I didn't remember ever being conscious of his hurting me in this way. It was always a surprise to me afterward that in my excitement I hadn't noticed, and I surveyed bruises at my throat or on my thighs with the sweetest regret. Now I struggled to lift my shoulders, for they were fast being rubbed raw against the carpet. Pascal held me down. I couldn't tell how excited he was; he had become silent and rhythmic and his face was hidden against my shoulder.

"Pascal," I said. "Please. You're hurting me."

Still he didn't stop. It struck me that I had never complained to him before but that I had always assumed if I did he would stop at once. It was part of the game, I thought, but now I saw it wasn't a game at all. Suddenly everything hurt, every place where our bodies touched was a zone of pain, my arms and legs ached, there was a dreadful ringing in my ears, but most of all, deep inside, there was a dry, throbbing, agonizing pain that made me want to scream, and I thought that if Pascal didn't stop in the next moment I would scream.

I turned my face toward his shoulder and bit him as hard as I could. He tried to shake me loose but I held on. Raising us both up, he caught me about the neck and pressed his thumb into my throat until I was forced to release him. I saw his face then. He looked excited and annoyed at once. I braced my hands against his chest and tried to push him off, but this only served to vex him. He caught my wrists in one hand and pulled my arms up over my head. Then he pressed his forearm across my throat with such force that I cried out. I could neither move nor breathe, and as I lay gasping for air I understood that only one thing would relieve my suffering and so I brought my legs up around his back and held on as if my life depended on it. Christ, I thought, let him come.

The sounds from my throat grew louder and louder. I could hear nothing else and there was a curious tingling in my arms and legs that mystified me. Pascal moaned again and lifted himself above me so that I knew it was almost over. I tried to look at him but it was as if a curtain of red were being drawn and withdrawn across my eyes. He looked down at me just as this curtain closed for the last time. I felt the harsh rush of air as he lifted his arm from my throat and I knew that my hands were free and that my back, which was bleeding, was being pulled up from the carpet and that Pascal was calling my name in a voice that was terror-stricken, but it was all too late. The red had darkened to black and it was to this blackness that I willingly surrendered my consciousness.

TWENTY-FOUR

WHEN I came to, I was lying on the bed. Pascal was bending over me. There was a cold washcloth on my forehead and he was rubbing my hands between his own with a look of such nervous, grandmotherly concern that I smiled. I was cold and I tried to tell him but the effort hurt my throat so badly that tears filled my eyes.

Pascal lifted me carefully and brought a glass of water to my lips. I swallowed it as best I could. "I'm cold," I said when I had had enough.

He set the glass on the nightstand and helped me pull the bedspread back. When I moved it hurt my back and arms. I stretched out under the spread carefully, flinching when my back touched the cool sheets. Pascal sat beside me, adjusting the covers about my shoulders.

"Will you be all right?" he said.

I turned on my side. "I feel as if I've been in a car crash," I said.

"I didn't know I was hurting you."

"I think I told you," I replied.

"I didn't know," he repeated.

I looked at him curiously. How could he say he didn't know? And why was he being so careful not to apologize? "Why did you do that?" I insisted.

"I would never . . ." he said, taking my hand. He kissed my palm, then closed my fingers and gazed at the fist he had made. "You bring that out in me."

So it was to be my fault, I thought. "You're a bastard," I hissed.

"I got carried away," he protested. "Usually you like that sort of thing. And it's been so long."

"But I asked you to stop."

"I asked you if you were all right."

I looked at him incredulously. I had no memory of his asking this question. "No you didn't," I said.

He sat up straight. "I did. I asked you if you were all right and you said you were."

"Stop it," I said. "Stop lying. I'm not going to take the blame for your trying to strangle me."

"Emma," he said, "I never wanted to hurt you. I thought you wanted me to."

"Right," I said. "You don't enjoy it at all."

"It's not that," he said. He looked away at the carpet and though he appeared to avert his eyes from shame I noticed at the corner of his mouth the nervous play of an inappropriate smile.

"That was the best orgasm you ever had in your life, wasn't it?" I said.

The smile deepened, but he couldn't look at me.

"Wasn't it?" I said again.

Still he didn't speak.

"I wish I'd been there to see it," I said.

He turned to me. "Do you think a warm bath would help you?" he asked. "Or would it make you feel worse?"

"I think it would help," I said.

"Do you want me to get you something to drink or eat?"

"If we went on, how long do you think it would be before you killed me?"

"If we went on?" he asked. He brushed my hair away from my face and exchanged with me a long, sad look. I thought he had brutalized me past caring, but now I saw that I would never be past caring for him.

"I love you," he said, after a moment. "When I'm without you . . ." He paused.

I reached up to touch his cheek. Even this small motion hurt so that I winced. Pascal continued to look at me. I felt he saw in me something that passed comprehension and I believed that he loved me for that, or in spite of that, I didn't know which. At last he stood up and his features took on that busy concern which often charmed me. "I'll run your bath for you," he said. "And then I'll go get something for you. Whatever you want. Do you want some champagne? Can you get champagne in this ghetto?"

"Yes," I said. "That would be great."

He disappeared into the bathroom, then came out again. He kissed me carefully. "I'll be right back," he said, and he went out.

I sat up in the bed and put my feet on the floor. I thought of Claire. I didn't have a vision of her, but I thought of her. I knew all at once, as if the information came to me through the floor, what I had done and what I would do. I had been successful in love, through love. I had found the love that would put an end to me, created a bond that was stronger than my will, and I couldn't break it. What Claire said she wanted, I had: a lover who would consume me entirely.

I have read that repentance is the act by which we put the past behind us, and if that is true, at that moment I repented of ever having loved, touched, wanted Pascal. I repented myself of it all. All I wanted was to be free of this passion. I crossed the room and turned off the bath water. Then I put on my clothes quickly. My shirt lay in a heap on the floor, and when I picked it up I noticed two spots of blood on the carpet. The sight filled me with such sadness that I stood looking at it. It was still raining; the light in the room was extraordinarily bright. I was utterly alone; my loneliness made me tremble. I looked up at the window, where the rain streaked down like tears. After a moment I pulled on my shoes and left. I walked down the long corridor to an elevator I thought Pascal would be unlikely to use.

On the street I unlocked my bike and rode a few blocks in the direction of my house, but I had such difficulty keeping my balance that I stopped, lay the bike on its side in the street, and sat down on the curb. I felt wonderfully numb, perfectly empty. It was a bad neighborhood for a woman to be in alone but I didn't care. If someone wanted to hurt me, I thought, let them do it now and get it over with. But no one came out of the shadows that flickered with the light of the street fires, no one cared to accost me. I fell into a reverie, recalling, for no reason I could explain, the day Claire and I had stood beside the river and surveyed the dying army of rats. I thought of my daughter's innocent hand in mine, of Claire's innocent figure at my side. The sight of so much suffering had shocked me into innocence, so that we were leveled by what we saw. Horror drew us together. It was an idea that explained to me the deadly fascination some people have for horror.

My mind was ablaze with hope, a condition I knew to be indicative of an imminent flood of hopelessness. I knew that Pascal would be too proud, or too understanding, to pursue me now, that I had cut him off in such a way that any reconciliation would have to be initiated by me.

After a while I got up and pedaled my way home. When I threw myself upon my bed, hours later, it was with one thought. "What have I done?" I cried aloud, pulling my own hair as if I could pull out the memory of Pascal. "What have I done?"

TWENTY-FIVE

P ASCAL was right: the quarantine didn't last much longer. It was November and the air was cool, though not unseasonably so. The daily death counts had been between one and four for some time. Then, one week after Pascal crossed the quarantine, the count shot to fifteen. There was a general panic. Some citizens stormed the National Guardsmen, who had come to despise those they guarded and turned their rifles on them with gusto. Hasty meetings were called inside and outside the quarantine and our city strained like an amoeba attempting to eject something large and indigestible.

In the end it was money that decided our fate. The state of Louisiana was nearly bankrupt and had failed to compensate our captors for an entire month. The next month without pay came and went during our panic, and after a few days of sniping and exchanging hand-to-hand blows with hecklers, the Guardsmen put down their rifles and walked away. The city was open again.

Many people left at once but as many stayed, carrying on much as they had before. The city government was unable to find anyone who would agree to work for nothing, which was what they had in their coffers. They employed one another and held numerous meetings. It was as if they didn't know they were powerless.

I didn't see Pascal day after day and I began to conceive of a life without him. But it was such a tedious, empty life that I couldn't care for it, and longed for him. Yet I believed my decision to be final and perfectly justified as well, so I continued without him.

It was difficult to be alone, especially at night. I could get through the days pretty easily, but after Chris was asleep and my house lay quiet all around me, I couldn't find anything to do but be afraid. In the darkness all the unpleasant creatures appeared, from inside reason and without. My house had mice, geckos, big roaches, and moths, a harmless group, to be sure, but in a still house they can make a terrific racket.

My head had Pascal. I kept a journal, a treatise on my lost love affair. When I longed for his arms, his eyes, for some little endearment he was given to—the way he had of touching my sleeve, as if the material were precious for being next to my skin, the wholehearted approval he showed whenever I ate all my dinner, his habit of steering me through crowds by my elbow, silly, meaningless gestures that touched me to the heart—whenever I found myself brooding over these, I turned to my journal and recalled, for my own instruction, the practical reasons for having left him.

These reasons had a way of ringing pretty hollow at about two A.M., tot them up though I might. My efforts made me increasingly miserable. I tried, as much as a wounded ego can, to be honest with myself, but of course at first all I could think of was that Pascal was often faithless, sometimes cruel, and that he had humiliated me. Only gradually did I discover that, though these were clear symptoms of the real trouble, like many another silly woman I probably could have learned to create excuses for these failings (or just ignored them) had it not been for the deep and abiding cynicism that was, after all, the real quality about Pascal that I couldn't tolerate.

I knew this was true because as the days passed my head began to clear and I felt a peculiar, unexpected freedom. Pascal's cynicism had rubbed off on me; I had even gone so far as occasionally to admire the eloquence with which he expressed his contempt for absurdities like nationalism, psychoanalysis, or fundamentalism. I'm not suggesting that without Pascal I became idealistic, or that I began to cherish even the vaguest optimism about the future of our poor planet. I felt only that I could entertain all sorts of possibilities, that I was not so eager to dismiss every idea that threatened me, that I could contemplate the enormous suffering of all living things with something approaching the real sympathy that they deserve, the awful, deep sadness that must precede our release from this fascinating life.

In fact, though I missed Pascal, though I was lonely and often frustrated, I enjoyed periods of intense receptivity, when my senses were all on the alert and the world poured in freely, without suffering alteration from the twin filters of judgment and doubt.

TWENTY-SIX

CLAIRE'S exile from her convent was drawing to its natural close and she was eager to return. Her mother was, as usual, in agreement with her, doubtless because she was concerned for her daughter's physical well-being and there was no plague north of the lake. Father Paine and the mother-general of the convent exchanged letters on the subject. They discussed whether Claire might well serve a useful purpose by staying on in the city. Father Paine's letters contained two interesting omissions. He failed to describe the small but intense following that Claire had inspired in his superstitious congregation. He also did not mention a more serious matter, perhaps because he wasn't certain how to mention it: the spiritual impasse Claire had come to.

"It's as if I'd crossed a street," she told him, "and on one side the sun was pouring down and the air was sweet and everything was given. But this side is so dark, it's absolutely dreary, there are creatures lurking in the shadows, and I pray and pray, just to see one little ray of light somewhere, just to breathe one little breath of air that isn't fetid and full of horror. Everywhere I look I see myself. I find myself crying in public for no reason. It's disgusting."

"You're depressed," the priest offered. "Who wouldn't be, living as you do?"

"I can't pray!" she exclaimed. "And when I do, I'm praying to go backward, to be what I was."

"You can't go back, Claire," he said. "Experience of the world is changing you and you're frightened. It's perfectly natural."

"Oh, natural," she moaned. "Next thing you'll tell me I'm getting my period."

The priest blushed and looked down at his hands, which rested on the table between them. Claire's directness embarrassed him and he could think of no adequate response. "No," he said at last, "I don't think that."

Claire got up abruptly and faced the long window looking out on the garden. "I'm impatient with everything," she said. "I feel so agitated all the time."

"I know," the priest said. "I can see that."

"Can't you help me?" she said, turning to him.

"No," he said. "I can't help you. No one can help you. You'll just have to wait. The question is where? There's work for you here and quiet for you in Lacombe. Which do you need most?"

Claire returned to her chair and sat with her head resting between her hands, the picture of dull despair. "I want to go back," she pleaded. "More than anything, right now. I want to go back. But I want to go for all the wrong reasons. I'm afraid of what's happening to me and I want to escape, to be safe. It's cowardice that makes me want to leave." She paused, considering her options. "But I'm afraid that if I stay I'll give scandal to everyone who knows me, because I'm so anxious and" — she faltered — "because I can't even pray anymore."

"It's ridiculous to worry about that part," the priest replied. "You're not here to make impressions on people, and God doesn't need your help to look attractive."

Claire laughed. "Of course," she said. "You're right."

"What worries me, Claire, is this. Suppose you do go back to Lacombe, suppose you're protected in the convent routine and you've got nothing to do but take care of your soul, and then suppose this aridity you're suffering from doesn't get any better. It can last a long time, you know. It can last for years."

Claire said nothing. She gazed at her confessor and he looked back at her with pure sympathy, for he had been where she was and he had a clear idea of what she was about to go through. After a long moment, Claire looked away. "Oh, Lord," she said.

"Let me write to Mother Grace one more time," he said. "Stay here until she answers. Keep working as you have. And do this too."

Claire looked up, a patient eager for any prescription.

"Try to remember exactly when you began to have this difficulty. See if there wasn't something you observed, or something someone said, something particular that may have caused you to feel . . . as you do."

"All right," she said. "I'll try."

"And then just concentrate on being someone who is waiting."

"I'll try," she said again, but she looked as if it was an onerous task.

"Patiently waiting," the priest cautioned her. "There's nothing God finds more pleasing."

———

TWENTY-SEVEN

Claire waited quietly, as if this important decision were of no concern to her. She worked in the hospital, where we were often together, but we were both so busy and so preoccupied with our personal struggles that we did little more than exchange pleasantries. I was learning not to think of Pascal, a lesson I couldn't enjoy. Claire was learning to wait, but still she implored her Creator for some sign, some evidence of His preference in her case. Either He had none or He preferred her to make up her own mind, for though she spent hours on her knees she felt she was kneeling before a closed door. She knew her Lord never turned away an honest supplicant and that the door was hinged in only one direction. Somehow she had closed it on herself. She struggled in vain to answer Father Paine's parting question: When had this aridity begun? Then one cool, autumn afternoon the answer came and knocked at the door of her house.

When her mother told her that a Mr. Toussaint was waiting to see her, Claire's first thought was that Pascal's father had come after another trying dinner engagement. She went down the stairs doggedly, thinking that the quarantine had provided certain distinct advantages. Her mother's house had a double parlor, divided by sliding oak doors that were unceremoniously closed whenever uninvited guests came to call. Claire stood for a moment smoothing her hair back, looking down at the line of light that poured over the carpet through the narrow opening. Her mother had disappeared into the kitchen, and the house seemed still and cold behind her. She grasped the two handles and shoved the big panels apart. Pascal, who was sitting in a blue velvet chair directly in front of her, stood up and advanced a step in her direction. "Claire," he said, "I hope I'm not disturbing you."

She stood looking at him, her hands still grasping the old brass door handles. It was within her power simply to close the doors again and return to the quiet of her bedroom. Perhaps this thought crossed her mind, for she hesitated a long moment before she stepped inside, turned, and closed the doors resolutely on her final interview with Pascal.

How many times and in what guises have I tried to imagine myself on the other side of those doors. What incredible motives have I assigned to both parties for staying together quietly over an hour. My poor desperate ego has even conceived the possibility that they were talking about me. But I guess in vain, conjure up the scene pointlessly, for finally I am face to face with the immensity of my own ignorance. I don't know why Pascal went to see Claire. I don't know what he wanted. Did he visit her with the intention of seducing her, if not into his arms, at least into his influence, or was it possible that he sought her out as she had once sought me out, with no particular intention beyond a dull craving for resolution?

And Claire, whose repugnance for Pascal was such that

she considered his conversation dangerous to her eternal salvation, why was she, in her anxious, exhausted state, willing to entertain his thorough skepticism of everything she held dear? Pascal had once reduced her to a sniveling hysteric and parted from her by flinging her own proud words in her face. Did she think, as she listened to him, that here was the answer to her question and the end of her indecision? Had she, then, been waiting only for the opportunity to vindicate herself?

I stand with my head bowed against those closed doors. Eventually Claire came out, went to her room, and fell to her knees before her crucifix. Pascal went out as he had come, back to the life he had always known, before he knew anything of Claire or of me.

Claire said nothing about her conversation with Pascal, not to her mother, who noticed only that she appeared unaccountably cheerful after his visit, nor to her confessor. Apparently it was not, in her view, an occasion of even potential sin. Her agitation and gloom mysteriously vanished, and she appeared the next morning at the hospital in high spirits. I was in good form myself (though if I had known then of Pascal's visit, I imagine my mood would have been abruptly altered), and even our kindhearted, plodding Father Paine admitted that the cool, perfect autumn air outside filled him with optimism. It was a foolish notion, but we all believed that hot weather somehow increased the possibility of the plague spreading its feverish, devastating arms around our population and that one good, cold, wet New Orleans winter would deliver us from its dehydrating grip.

The three of us went out to lunch, and it was during that pleasant meal that Claire's future was settled. In a volley of letters both the mother-general of the convent and Father Paine had finally agreed that Claire was to return to the mother house as soon as possible. At this news Claire breathed a great sigh of relief. She turned to her confessor with the mock solemnity that was one of her peculiar charms, patting him on the hand like a consoling mother. "All I have to say about that," she told him, "is thank Christ."

"Well, don't thank Him too soon," the priest responded. "Now we've got to figure out how to get you there."

Claire returned her attention to the greasy grilled-cheese sandwich in front of her. "It's not a problem," she said. "I'll walk."

"You can get a bus to the north shore," Father Paine said. "There's one running both ways now. But that leaves twenty miles to Lacombe."

"I walk twenty miles every day," Claire replied. It was true. We were all accustomed to going by foot. Jane Austen's cosmography made perfect sense to me then. If you wanted to see someone, you put on walking shoes.

"But that's walking around the city, where you know your way," the priest protested. "This is twenty miles of highway, through the woods, and there's no one around."

"Considering the neighborhood I come through every day," Claire replied, "I doubt that I'll be in unusual danger."

"That's true," I agreed.

"Maybe we can have someone come out to meet you."

Claire frowned at him, licking the butter from her fingertips. His caution amused her. She answered him with a bit of the stunning wisdom of Carmel, a sentence that was to ring in my ears with brutal irony for many months to come. "To reach that which you do not know," she said, "you must travel by a way you do not know."

TWENTY-EIGHT

B EFORE she left, Claire wrote a letter to Father Paine.

"For the moment," she wrote, "all my difficulties are behind me. I seem foolish to myself, with my constant quibbling, my concentration on trying to *be* something or get something or show forth something, wasting enormous energy on wanting rather than simply being. When this period of calm set in I discovered anew something I've always known: desire keeps love away, stillness brings love pouring in. I think of what you told me, that God likes nothing better than to see a soul patiently waiting, and I want to change that 'waiting,' so full of expectancy and need, to 'being still.' So I admonish myself a thousand times a day (and I try to do it affectionately, without undue agitation), 'Just be still.'

"Your advice and help have been invaluable to me. Will you, as you promised, write to me in Lacombe? I don't want to bind you to the routine I've kept you in these last months, victim of my daily, dreary, repetitious confessions. At times I've felt guilty and imagined that it must be quite a burden, this never-ending drama of my conscience. (I've felt guilty for being guilty.) And sometimes I fear I've only exposed you to the panorama of my moods and kept the matter of my soul (which isn't, after all, a mood, no matter how much it may feel that way) hidden from your view. My consolation has often been that it is your *job* to listen and it is my job to be penitent, so that if I was honest and you were listening closely, we have at least done what is required of us. Hard work, this business of serving God.

"Another difficulty I've often suffered is my fear that what I want from my vocation isn't virtue but some experience of another reality. I've never for a moment been able to believe that a lifetime of struggling to earn a living, acquire the right house and friends, raise children, could provide me with anything but the purest frustration, so the religious life offers an obvious escape for me. What I find as I make my slow, stumbling progress in prayer and meditation is that I was absolutely right: there is indeed another reality, and that it is somewhat frightening because it requires the total surrender of my will and finally, ultimately, the wholesale destruction of my ego. This is hard. If I'm going into another world, I cry out, I want to be *me* in it.

"What I've learned in the last months, perhaps in the last weeks, thanks largely to this forced immersion in our city, so stricken with every kind of plague (moral, psychological, physical), is that prayer can be a goal outside the world, that learning to pray, like learning to make music, breaks down the will and the ego because it is so difficult to do it properly and it requires such total concentration. The world and Claire go away. And of course, as with music, one can never become so accomplished at prayer that there's nothing more to learn.

"My metaphor is a foolish one. I am a novice at these matters. When I look down the years I know my way of seeing will be much altered before anything resembling clarity comes to me.

"I leave tomorrow at eight. Thank you for your help in this difficult year.

"Yours in Christ,
"Claire"

TWENTY-NINE

THE MORNING of Claire's departure arrived, and
at her request I rose early to walk with her to the bus stop
on Canal Street. She was in good spirits. She looked forward to the long walk and to her destination. She talked
of how much good it had done her to be away so long, of
how the year she had passed in the city had proved useful
to her, of how she had improved, and I wondered if perhaps
her greatest accomplishment in this time hadn't been to
separate me from Pascal. I was bitter but I didn't blame
her. I liked the bright looks she cast about her, as if she
planned to store the memory of what she saw. She inquired
about Chris and about my husband.

"Will you return to him?" she asked.

"No," I said, "I don't think so."

"But you should."

I laughed. "How would you know? You hardly know
him. He might be a very bad husband."

"Even so," she said.

"I'm still in love with Pascal."

She was startled by this confession. We hadn't spoken
of Pascal for weeks. The morning after I parted from him
I had told her that I wouldn't see him again. She hadn't
inquired into my reasons.

"I didn't know that," she said. We walked on without talking. She was abstracted, but I thought I knew the subject of her thoughts. A cold voice within me appreciated her turmoil. She could not, I judged, understand my feelings about her or about Pascal in a thousand years. I didn't understand them myself. So I imagined myself superior to her, more complicated, hence more interesting. When we arrived at the stop, the bus stood waiting, its winglike doors folded open. She took my hand in her own to say goodbye, and I looked into her mild eyes.

"I've caused you pain, and I'm sorry for it," she said. "But perhaps that pain will keep you from forgetting me."

And leaving me with this queer sentiment, she released me and hurried into the waiting bus. I stood on the sidewalk and waved to her through the window as the bus pulled away.

I never saw her again.

THIRTY

THE ROAD was wide, black asphalt, and because so few cars used it now grass and small shrubs had sprung up in the many cracks. The forest on either side was thick, primordial, so densely packed with vines and thorny plants that Claire couldn't see into it. She walked along quietly, her eyes moving over the road ahead of her. It was a cold day, but she was warm from exercise and she unbuttoned her coat, pushing it back from her chest. She had fallen into a pure and serene state of mind. She considered the complexity and beauty of the nature around her and thought with affection of the hand that had formed it, the mind that imagined it, the heart that loved it still. A mockingbird filled the air with every conversation he had heard for a week; some had been bitter, others, Claire thought, were surely war cries. One was a confession of deep sorrow. She stopped to look at the drab creature pouring his lovely song upon the still air. Then she turned and looked back down the road.

She had walked over fifteen miles. She knew the road now; she would arrive at the gates of the convent in less than an hour. Her heart lifted as she stood there, so close to the place where she believed she would find peace of mind. She was impatient to be there but still she stood looking back. "It's all behind me now," she said. The bird paid no attention to her. He had arrived in his song at a concluding rapture. She smiled as she looked up at him again.

There were two men walking toward her, one on either side of the road. She couldn't tell where they had come from, perhaps from the forest. They strode toward her purposefully, scarcely a hundred feet ahead. One, she saw, was heavy, very large; the other she thought she recognized, the convent gardener, and she smiled, but then he was closer and she saw that she didn't know him. She took a step toward them. They had come up together on the road and were very near her. The reality of her situation, alone on a road miles from anyone who knew her, dawned on her abruptly and she was afraid. She tried to conquer her fear by meeting the eyes of the smaller, darker man and saying hello.

He smiled without speaking and looked at his friend. For a moment Claire thought they meant to pass her without speaking, but just as he was even with her shoulder the smaller man turned and caught her hard by the arm, pulling her toward him with such force that she stumbled against him. The big man was on her at once, and the other had to step aside. He knocked her to her knees on the pavement and pulled her hair back so that her face was turned toward his own. She cried out and tried with her free hand to push away the other man, who knelt before her, pushing her coat back and tearing open the front of her blouse. The big man slapped her, most of the blow landing on her ear, then pulled her back harder so that her cheek touched the scratchy material of his shirt. She kept her eyes opened and struggled with all her strength, but she was no match for the two of them. The big man put his forearm across her neck, choking her cruelly. Her back was pressed against his stomach, her hands pinioned behind her. She tried to kick the other man away, but he caught her legs at the knees and pushed them apart impatiently. The pressure at her throat was intolerable; she could hear the sound of her own desperate spasmodic breathing everywhere in her head. She looked wildly at the man who attacked her, who now cursed her and attempted to hold her flailing legs with one arm while with the other he drew, from inside a long leather sheath at his side, a gleaming knife as long as her own arm and as sharp as the pain in her constricted lungs.

THIRTY-ONE

LATE that evening Claire's mother phoned the convent to make sure her daughter had reached her destination. The mother-general told her that Claire had not arrived. They were worried. She should have been there by seven, and it was now ten-thirty. Claire's mother tried to remain calm, but by the time she concluded the phone call she was in a panic. She then called Father Paine. The news of Claire's disappearance struck him with the force of a confirmation. As he hurried along the streets to her mother's house he thought he had known that something terrible was going to happen. The police were informed, and two officers came to the house to fill out a questionnaire. Claire had planned to have a late lunch at Mr. Richard's Restaurant on the north shore of the lake. Father Paine called Mr. Richard, who said he had seen Claire earlier that day. She had come in, flushed from her walk, tired and very hungry. She had eaten half a loaf of French bread, a green salad, some cheddar cheese, and a glass of milk. "If you're hungry," Mr. Richard had told her, "why don't you let me make you a po'boy. I got some fine oysters." But she had refused.

After Father Paine phoned him, Mr. Richard couldn't stop thinking of Claire. He finished closing his restaurant, phoned his wife to explain his mission, called his big hunting dog from his slumber on the back porch, and, taking a flashlight and a hunting knife, set off down the road in the direction of Lacombe. He walked for nearly an hour without finding any sign of her. The night was cold and damp, and the stars glittered in the black sky overhead. He could smell the sweet scent of pine trees and of the dark, moist soil. Abruptly his dog shot ahead of him, ran ten yards or so, then stopped, sniffing the air anxiously. Mr. Richard cast his flashlight, as he had been doing for some time, back and forth across the road. This time the small circle of light discovered something that stopped him in his tracks. At the edge of the road he saw a hand extended toward him, the fingers splayed and caked with dried blood. He ran ahead in the dark night, giving a little cry as he played the small beam of his flashlight across the rest of Claire's body.

He had not known her, but he had seen her alive a few hours earlier, and the sight of her mutilated body was more than he could bear. The old dog fell to nervous whimpering as his master sat down on the road next to her corpse, too weak and too saddened to stand. Her clothes lay torn and scattered all about, on the road and on the grass. She had been left face down, her pale skin covered everywhere with a mat of dirt, grass, and blood. Mr. Richard couldn't turn her over; he was afraid to see her face.

He judged that he was a little closer to the convent than to his restaurant, so, when he stood up again, he went on ahead. It was his duty, he thought, to make sure her family was informed as soon as possible, that those who loved her should know she was entirely and eternally lost to them.

* * *

Early the next morning, just before daybreak, the Cathedral bell began to toll. Those few who were up at that hour wondered to hear it, for it tolled so slowly, so mournfully, and for such a long time that the sound weighed the air like a child's sighing. Who had died? they asked, and some consulted newspaper headlines to see if perhaps it was someone important.

The sexton at the Cathedral stood in the yard; he had yielded his post to Father Paine. He looked up at the tower, reflecting that it sounded very different in the open air, that it was not, as he knew it, deep and deafening, but clear and strangely touching.

Inside the Cathedral, in the dark bell tower, the priest bent to his lonely work. It comforted him to pull the heavy rope, to hear the whining and clicking of the mechanism and, finally, the great shock as the clapper struck the giant bell. In his heart he cursed the world and all the living ears that might hear his lament. When he had watched Claire's mother replacing the phone in the receiver, her eyes watching her own hand, he had felt his mouth go dry. He couldn't stay with her because, he told himself as he staggered down the stairs of her house, there was a sense in which Claire had been his own daughter; hers was the young life he had wanted to protect, to comfort, as a father comforts his daughter, with the only love she will ever know that is blind to her faults. He pulled the rope and let it slip up through his hands and pulled it again. He wanted to weep, but no tears came. He thought of Christ, Claire's beloved, Who had tantalized the world with her and called her back too soon, and he knew that he hated Christ, had always hated Him, that any service was better than His thankless, endless service, that His love was the hectic, worrying love of a despot.

At last the sexton came in and tried to pry the priest from the rope. Father Paine pushed the man away, clung to the rope, but after a brief struggle he gave in and allowed himself to be led away. He went into his kitchen and sat silently at his table. After a while he got up and threw the camellias in the bowl before him into the trash can. Then he sat down again.

THIRTY-TWO

I LEARNED of Claire's death that afternoon, when I phoned her mother's house. By that time a distant relative, whose grief was not deepened by having had any acquaintance with Claire, had been dispatched to the phone. This person told me that Claire would be buried at the convent the following morning. I tried to carry on with an ordinary day, but by evening I gave it up. I wanted to tell Pascal and I wanted to do it at once. I didn't know why it seemed so important to me that he should know, but I could literally think of nothing else. My last conversation with Claire had been about Pascal, and I think I hated him for that. I set out on the long bus trip to to his apartment without thinking of what I would do if he wasn't at home, or if there was another woman with him, or if, somehow, he already knew what I wanted to tell him.

He was at home, alone, and when he opened the door and looked at me he didn't seem displeased to see me. Then he remembered our last meeting, and that memory settled between us like a fog. "What is it?" he asked.

"Claire's dead," I said. "She was killed on the road."

"Emma," he said, disbelieving me.

"She was walking back to the convent. She was stabbed to death."

He saw that I was telling the truth and, as I watched, that truth took hold of him. He didn't move, but every line of him was altered; he seemed to sink into the floor. He stepped back into the room, leaving the door ajar. I followed him inside. He put one hand over his mouth and sat down hard on the couch. His shoulders slumped forward; his breath caught in his throat and made a harsh, rasping sound. Then he began to cry. "Please go," he said through his tears, and he made a feeble dismissing gesture with his hand. But I couldn't go. There was something fascinating about the sight of him. "Please," he said again. "Can't you leave me alone?"

It was guilt, I decided. He believed he had wronged her. "I'm sorry," I said. I went out hurriedly, having done what I had intended to do.

Later we learned the painful details. Claire's face had been so badly battered that she was waked in a closed coffin. The knife blade had broken against her bones, but this had not stopped her attackers from continuing their assault. There was no doubt that she had fought for her life. Enough of her assailants' skin, hair, and blood was scraped from beneath her fingernails and between her teeth to effect a positive identification of them. They were apprehended some weeks later. Both pled guilty and recalled their crime in the court for the titillation of the newspaper reporters, whose pens moved busily for days to come.

I didn't go to the funeral. A few weeks later I walked from the city to the convent and back again. My husband, who discouraged me from this trip but finally gave in, equipped me with a small pistol, which I carried in my hand all the way.

I set out early, taking the bus from downtown, through the sprawling, ugly suburbs and across Lake Pontchartrain. As I stepped down into the cool morning air, I was surprised to see a truck coming toward the city from the northern shore. The gasoline situation, we were told, was steadily improving, but this unexpected vehicle was the first proof I had seen of it.

I sat down on the grass and ate the sandwich I had made that morning. I looked back across the dark water as I ate, and it seemed to me that the waves broke against one another with powerful malevolence. The sky began to clear and I was treated to a fine natural spectacle, the clouds thinning, the sun's rays breaking through and sweeping the black water with silver, the dissolving of cheerless gloom into unexpected beauty. Sea gulls swooped down, screaming with glee as they plucked gleaming edibles from the waves. At last I got up and went on, planning to stop, as Claire had, at Mr. Richard's Restaurant.

This proved to be a small frame house, set up on piers, with a long sagging screened porch across both the front and back. Inside I found one large room cluttered with tables. Patrons occupied several of these; a few more sat at the bar behind which Mr. Richard himself stood grinning. I took my seat at a table and he came out from behind the bar, bustling with a water glass, flatware, and menu, all intended for me.

"Are you Mr. Richard?" I asked when I had ordered a beer and a portion of boiled shrimp.

"I am," he said cheerfully. "Do I know you?"

"No," I said. "I'm a friend of Claire's. The young woman you found . . ."

An expression of extreme trouble clouded his features, compressing his lips and knitting his brow so intently that I wished I hadn't spoken. He was clearly of a nature that could and would forget unhappiness whenever possible and for whom the memory of sorrow was as powerful as the original experience. "That poor child," he said. "Are you going to visit her grave?"

This question caught me unaware. I had thought to create some peace of mind for myself by repeating Claire's last walk, for I found I thought of it, of her, too often. That I meant to stand at her grave, this was a new idea to me, but I saw at once that I did mean to. "Yes," I said. "I thought I would."

"I only went once," he said. "For the funeral. You know the way?"

"I think so," I said. "It's right on the highway, isn't it?"

"Well, there's a turn-off, but there's a sign." He paused in preparation for a more personal remark. "It was about an hour from here," he said. "I don't walk too fast, though; you might go faster. But if you look at your watch you can tell about where and if you look on the right side of the road you'll see" — he paused again, then finished hurriedly — "the place where her blood soaked into the road."

We looked away from each other. He returned to his station behind the bar; I looked out the window at the tall rain trees that shaded the yard outside. I thought of Claire's last words to me and couldn't help agreeing that the trouble she had caused me would keep her alive in my imagination.

Later, I looked at my watch as I set off from Mr. Richard's Restaurant. It seemed to me that the character of my expedition had changed, and I thought of returning, though I knew there was no way to go back then. I was, I told myself, only weary from walking, from the beer I had drunk, from the sensation Mr. Richard had unwittingly given me that mine was a morose adventure at best. I glanced at my watch repeatedly. The air was still. It was that hour before evening when the sun sheds great horizontal beams just above the horizon and the air itself reveals levels of dust and insect life previously unthought of. I began to scan nervously the right side of the highway, hoping that I would pass, without noticing it, the spot on which Claire had died. It seemed to me that the road was covered with patches of discoloration, that generations of animals and men had met their death on it. I saw a large spot that was not like the others, not so faded. The stain was different, a brownish orange at the edge, where the road was light, a deeper color toward the center. Was this the place? I stopped. The air was cool, and the birds, who didn't regard me, squabbled overhead in the pines. I looked up and down the road, holding my gun carelessly, for there was nothing out of the ordinary to see. Something caught my eye above the tree tops, and as I watched, a hawk hurtled upward, whirling and turning slowly and describing a great spire that rose into the blue sky. The natural beauty of the earth made it hard for me to consider the pathetic struggle of humans on the face of it. The great release of death, I thought, was not from bondage to our lovely planet—who could ever wish to leave this extraordinary place?—but from one another. As I stood in the place where Claire had died I understood Claire's horror of human intimacy, though I did not entirely share it. Even as I had these thoughts, I experienced a physical longing for Pascal, for the sweetness I had sometimes enjoyed in my intimacy with him, so acute that I pushed all my imaginings away, consulted my watch without marking it, and continued on my journey.

THIRTY-THREE

I ARRIVED at the convent at dusk. The gate was opened by a young nun who said she had been released from the evening service in order to wait for me. She watched without comment as I hid my small pistol in my purse; then she asked if I wanted to see Claire's grave at once or preferred to eat dinner and rest. Her manner was studied but gracious, and I realized, as I admitted that I was hungry, that I was not the first who had come to Claire's grave and that I was not expected to be the last. Walking resolutely along the black highway, I had not thought myself on a pilgrimage, but now, as I followed the nun across a courtyard and into the large refectory, I knew that I had traveled as a pilgrim travels, for the love of the dead.

I took my meal alone. The refectory was next to the chapel, and as I ate I could hear the nuns singing their evening service. Their high voices raised in plaintive chanting filled the air with such sweetness that, now and then, I put my fork down and closed my eyes. Claire's voice, I remember, had been clear and strong. It would have echoed purely with these others. That had been her great wish, to be where I was now, and I saw that there was, doubtless, an element of cruelty in those who had denied it to her.

I steeled my heart against the mother-general, whom, I knew, I would meet at the conclusion of these services.

A few minutes after the music stopped she entered the refectory. She was a tall, thin, plain woman; her face revealed little about her age or her disposition. She crossed the room ahead of her sisters, who came in single file, and she shook my hand perfunctorily before leading me down another hall to her office. She offered me a straight-back chair before taking for herself the more comfortable seat behind her desk.

"Did you know," she asked, "that Claire wrote to us about you?"

"No," I said.

She smiled. I had showed my surprise. "She wrote only to say that you were a friend to her. I don't get so much mail that I can't remember everything that's in it. She mentioned you, and when you called to say you were coming, I recognized your name."

"I was fond of her," I said. "We worked together during the quarantine." I stopped talking. The office was small and the nun had only opened the curtains, so that it grew darker every moment. She seemed to read my thoughts, for suddenly she reached out and switched on a floor lamp near her chair.

"Have you been to the grave yet?" she asked.

"No," I said. "I thought I'd wait until morning."

"You'll have plenty of time," she said. "You won't have to walk all the way back. There's a truck leaving Mr. Richard's Restaurant for the city at noon. Did he tell you?"

"No," I said.

"Perhaps he doesn't know it."

I thought her conversation strangely mechanical; I couldn't tell whether she took any pleasure in it or not. She opened a drawer next her and took out a stack of envelopes tied with a purple ribbon, which she set between us as if to tempt me closer.

"We've received a great many letters about Claire," she said. "As you can see." She toyed with the ribbon for a moment, then, as if on an impulse, pulled the bow loose. "I don't think there can be any harm in your seeing them."

"What do they say?" I asked, taking the bundle into my hands and glancing at the return address on the first letter.

"They testify to miracles for the most part," she said. "Performed publicly by Claire in her life and through her intercession now that she is dead."

"Miracles?" I said.

"Of course these claims will have to be investigated and verified one by one."

"To what end?" I asked.

"I'm afraid I don't know that yet," she replied. "I would suspect to no end at all." She looked at the letters in my hand as if, in spite of her professional skepticism, they were not entirely without promise for her. "Time will tell," she concluded.

I put the stack in my lap and chose one at random. It was from a woman in the city who claimed that Claire had tended her daughter in the hospital and that one evening the mother had noticed a certain luminosity about Claire's face and there issued, she claimed, from Claire's fingertips thin beams "like threads of gold." On that same evening Claire had told the woman that her daughter, who was universally acknowledged to be at death's door, would recover. By dawn the child had taken a sudden and inexplicable turn toward good health and was, at this very moment, entirely recovered and to be numbered, as Claire could no longer be, among the living.

I smiled as I read it. The mother's style was self-conscious; one could see through it her fear that, should she not tell her story properly, it would be dismissed as so much raving. The mother-general watched me as I read, her hands folded before her on her desk, her breathing, which was audible in the breathless silence of the convent, regular and slow. I returned the letter to its envelope and looked up at her before opening another. We exchanged a look of mild questioning, mine inquiring as to her intentions, hers inquiring, in a practiced, polished, and disarming way, into the state of my soul. Claire would have met that look, I thought, many times in her time as a postulant. It was, in some sense, to that look which she had hoped to return. I thumbed through the letters hopelessly, for whenever I thought of Claire I felt her image before me. I saw her as she had been that day on my porch, not so long ago. I remembered how she had lifted her eyebrows in astonishment at the thought of my willingness to change my life for Pascal, of how she had turned and moved her hand as if to touch me but then, on deeper thought, withdrawn it. Now she could no longer really be *found* in this life, not even in the convent she had longed to return to, and the memory of her filled me with such sadness that I discovered a tear slipping across the useless pile of letters in my lap. If there was one place she would never be found, I thought, it was in those letters.

To calm myself I bent a determined eye on the return addresses ranged before me. The name Toussaint flew out at me from one and I drew that letter quickly from the stack. A second glance revealed that it was not, as I feared, from Pascal, but from his father. I opened it and read it.

Mr. Toussaint, I read, was writing at the request of his pastor, Father Desmond James, to describe the miraculous delivery of his grandchild from the threatening, vicious, and deadly poisonous fangs of a snake. He had seen it all, he averred after a long, inflated description of the event itself, and it couldn't have been accomplished by a normal person. He didn't conclude, as the lady had, that Claire was a saint. He was content to proclaim her unnatural.

This letter annoyed me, and I folded it up as soon as I had read it and put it away from me. "I don't want to read these," I said, placing the stack back on the desk.

"I presume, then," she said, "you haven't come in order to add to our collection." She spoke sardonically, so that I felt myself suddenly within the range of her tolerance.

"No," I said. "She never performed any miracles when I knew her."

"Nor when I did," she said.

We were quiet for a moment. "Why," I asked at last, "did you send her back home?"

"I thought her too fervent," she said. "I was afraid for her. I couldn't discourage her myself . . ." She paused.

"But you thought the world would?"

"Yes," she said pleasantly. Then, gesturing impatiently at the letters, "I never expected anything like this to happen."

We smiled at each other. If Claire had ever hoped for this woman to take her seriously, I reflected, she was about to get her chance.

"I think I'd like to go to bed now," I said.

She rose from her seat. "You had a long, quiet, un-eventful walk, I hope."

"Yes," I said as we went out together. "Very quiet, very uneventful."

The next morning I rose early, breakfasted alone while the nuns prayed, and walked out to the community graveyard, which was behind the convent. Claire's grave was, like all the others, marked with a small marble cross on which was inscribed her name, the dates of her birth and death. Had she lived another month, I discovered, she would have been twenty-one. There were fresh flowers strewn across the ground beneath which she lay. I thought of her body, torn, rotting, and empty of her, and I had the sensation I often experience at the sight of a dead animal. Where, I wondered, had that animating force gone? What form would it take next? I remembered my daughter's birth and how, moments after her delivery, I had seen in her face an unexpected willfulness, exerting all her small strength to be free of me. This memory made me long for her small hand, her innocent eyes, her childish confidences, and I turned away and began to walk back to the city.

The day was bright and crisp as the one on which Claire had died. Again I stopped on the road and looked at the place where her blood had soaked into the pavement. I imagined that there were people who would think there was some justice in what had happened to her, that she had asked for it in some way, simply by being what she was. There is a sense, I suppose, in which innocence threatens experience and invites its own destruction. I knew it was none of her doing but rather in the nature of things. She possessed that quality we might make better use of in the future, an indomitable will turned inward. She cared to change no one else, but she would change herself, daily, hourly, into something better, stronger, paradoxically more obedient and more willful. She was fearless. She knew that when she met her death, whether she drifted into in her sleep or whether it was forced on her in the midst of her daily struggle for virtue, it would be the last test she must pass before she could have that union she most desired. For her sake I hoped such a union was more than the pipe dream it seemed to me as I stood on the spot where she had died. Then it struck me that I wanted to believe Claire had longed for something absurd and unattainable and that her struggle to have it was ultimately meaningless, for if Claire had failed, then my failure with Pascal was somehow easier to bear. Though, of course, I reflected, to any woman who wants from her lover only warmth, companionship, and respect, the notion that my liberation from Pascal constituted a failure on my part must be difficult to understand. Yet I couldn't rid myself of this feeling, rationalize though I might. I wouldn't go back to Pascal, but I wondered what would have happened if I had trusted him. Claire, without ever trying to, without probably any consciousness of having done so, simply by traveling for a little time through the same narrow atmosphere in which I traveled, had made that impossible for me. Claire was in my life now, as permanently as Pascal was out of it.

That, I confessed to myself, was a bold statement, and not entirely true. Though I had banished Pascal from my life, I couldn't escape him in my dreams. I dreamed of him constantly, and as I fell asleep, I often felt myself descending to the dark, airless chambers of my imagination, where he sat permanently enthroned, forever petulant and brooding, a king who rested his chin in his hands as he surveyed his ruined kingdom. In that sense, I suppose, the victory is his.

After a while I roused myself and walked on toward Mr. Richard's Restaurant. Hours later, when I got off the truck at Canal Street, it seemed to me that I had been away many days and that it was good to be back.

It's an odd sensation to recognize in oneself the need to be in a particular physical environment, when one longs for the home ground no matter how terrible the memories it holds, no matter how great the efforts made to leave it behind. So I have left this city again and again and thought myself lucky to escape its allure, for it's the attraction of decay, of vicious, florid, natural cycles that roll over the senses with their lushness. Where else could I find these hateful, humid, murderously hot afternoons, when I know that the past was a series of great mistakes, the greatest being the inability to live anywhere but in this swamp? I can't do without those little surges of joy at the sight of a chameleon, of a line of dark clouds moving in beneath the burning blue of the sky. I am comforted by the threatening encumbrance of moss on trees, the thick, sticky plantain trees that can grow from their chopped roots twenty feet in three months, the green scum that spreads over the lagoons and bayous, the colorful conversation of the lazy, suspicious, pleasure-loving populace. I don't think I will leave the city again.

The plague continues, neither in nor out of control, but we have been promised a vaccine that will solve all our problems. We go on without it, and life is not intolerable. Our city is an island, physically and psychologically; we are tied to the rest of the country only by our own endeavor. The river from which we drink drains a continent; it has to be purified for days before we can stomach it. We smile to ourselves when people from more fashionable centers find us provincial, for if we are free of one thing, it's fashion. The future holds a simple promise. We are well below sea level, and inundation is inevitable. We are content, for now, to have our heads above the water.

ABOUT THE AUTHOR

Valerie Martin is the author of the novels *A Recent Martyr,* *Alexandra* and *Set in Motion,* and the short-story collection *A Consolation of Nature and Other Stories.* She is currently at work on a new novel, *Mary Reilly.* She was born in Sedalia, Missouri, and grew up in New Orleans. Ms. Martin currently teaches at Mount Holyoke College in South Hadley, Massachusetts, where she resides with her daughter, Adrienne.

VINTAGE
CONTEMPORARIES

___ **Love Always** by Ann Beattie	$5.95	394-74418-7
___ **First Love and Other Sorrows** by Harold Brodkey	$7.95	679-72075-8
___ **The Debut** by Anita Brookner	$5.95	394-72856-4
___ **Cathedral** by Raymond Carver	$6.95	679-72369-2
___ **Fires** by Raymond Carver	$7.95	679-72239-4
___ **What We Talk About When We Talk About Love** by Raymond Carver	$5.95	679-72305-6
___ **Where I'm Calling From** by Raymond Carver	$8.95	679-72231-9
___ **Bop** by Maxine Chernoff	$5.95	394-75522-7
___ **I Look Divine** by Christopher Coe	$5.95	394-75995-8
___ **Dancing Bear** by James Crumley	$6.95	394-72576-X
___ **The Last Good Kiss** by James Crumley	$6.95	394-75989-3
___ **One to Count Cadence** by James Crumley	$5.95	394-73559-5
___ **The Wrong Case** by James Crumley	$5.95	394-73558-7
___ **The Last Election** by Pete Davies	$6.95	394-74702-X
___ **Great Jones Street** by Don DeLillo	$7.95	679-72303-X
___ **The Names** by Don DeLillo	$7.95	679-72295-5
___ **Players** by Don DeLillo	$6.95	679-72293-9
___ **Ratner's Star** by Don DeLillo	$8.95	679-72292-0
___ **Running Dog** by Don DeLillo	$6.95	679-72294-7
___ **A Narrow Time** by Michael Downing	$6.95	394-75568-5
___ **The Commitments** by Roddy Doyle	$6.95	679-72174-6
___ **From Rockaway** by Jill Eisenstadt	$6.95	394-75761-0
___ **Platitudes** by Trey Ellis	$6.95	394-75439-5
___ **Days Between Stations** by Steve Erickson	$6.95	394-74685-6
___ **Rubicon Beach** by Steve Erickson	$6.95	394-75513-8
___ **A Fan's Notes** by Frederick Exley	$7.95	679-72076-6
___ **Pages from a Cold Island** by Frederick Exley	$6.95	394-75977-X
___ **A Piece of My Heart** by Richard Ford	$6.95	394-72914-5
___ **Rock Springs** by Richard Ford	$6.95	394-75700-9
___ **The Sportswriter** by Richard Ford	$6.95	394-74325-3
___ **The Ultimate Good Luck** by Richard Ford	$5.95	394-75089-6
___ **Bad Behavior** by Mary Gaitskill	$6.95	679-72327-7
___ **Fat City** by Leonard Gardner	$6.95	394-74316-4
___ **Ellen Foster** by Kaye Gibbons	$5.95	394-75757-2
___ **Within Normal Limits** by Todd Grimson	$5.95	394-74617-1
___ **Airships** by Barry Hannah	$5.95	394-72913-7
___ **Dancing in the Dark** by Janet Hobhouse	$5.95	394-72588-3
___ **November** by Janet Hobhouse	$6.95	394-74665-1
___ **Saigon, Illinois** by Paul Hoover	$6.95	394-75849-8
___ **Angels** by Denis Johnson	$7.95	394-75987-7
___ **Fiskadoro** by Denis Johnson	$6.95	394-74367-9

VINTAGE
CONTEMPORARIES

___ **The Stars at Noon** by Denis Johnson	$5.95	394-75427-1
___ **Asa, as I Knew Him** by Susanna Kaysen	$4.95	394-74985-5
___ **Lulu Incognito** by Raymond Kennedy	$7.95	394-75641-X
___ **Steps** by Jerzy Kosinski	$5.95	394-75716-5
___ **A Handbook for Visitors From Outer Space** by Kathryn Kramer	$5.95	394-72989-7
___ **The Chosen Place, the Timeless People** by Paule Marshall	$6.95	394-72633-2
___ **A Recent Martyr** by Valerie Martin	$7.95	679-72158-4
___ **The Consolation of Nature and Other Stories** by Valerie Martin	$6.95	679-72159-2
___ **Suttree** by Cormac McCarthy	$6.95	394-74145-5
___ **California Bloodstock** by Terry McDonell	$7.95	679-72168-1
___ **The Bushwhacked Piano** by Thomas McGuane	$5.95	394-72642-1
___ **Nobody's Angel** by Thomas McGuane	$6.95	394-74738-0
___ **Something to Be Desired** by Thomas McGuane	$4.95	394-73156-5
___ **To Skin a Cat** by Thomas McGuane	$5.95	394-75521-9
___ **Bright Lights, Big City** by Jay McInerney	$5.95	394-72641-3
___ **Ransom** by Jay McInerney	$5.95	394-74118-8
___ **Story of My Life** by Jay McInerney	$5.95	679-72257-2
___ **Mama Day** by Gloria Naylor	$7.95	679-72181-9
___ **The All-Girl Football Team** by Lewis Nordan	$5.95	394-75701-7
___ **Welcome to the Arrow-Catcher Fair** by Lewis Nordan	$6.95	679-72164-9
___ **River Dogs** by Robert Olmstead	$6.95	394-74684-8
___ **Soft Water** by Robert Olmstead	$6.95	394-75752-1
___ **Family Resemblances** by Lowry Pei	$6.95	394-75528-6
___ **Norwood** by Charles Portis	$5.95	394-72931-5
___ **Clea & Zeus Divorce** by Emily Prager	$6.95	394-75591-X
___ **A Visit From the Footbinder** by Emily Prager	$6.95	394-75592-8
___ **Mohawk** by Richard Russo	$6.95	394-74409-8
___ **Anywhere But Here** by Mona Simpson	$6.95	394-75559-6
___ **Carnival for the Gods** by Gladys Swan	$6.95	394-74330-X
___ **The Player** by Michael Tolkin	$7.95	679-72254-8
___ **Myra Breckinridge and Myron** by Gore Vidal	$8.95	394-75444-1
___ **The Car Thief** by Theodore Weesner	$6.95	394-74097-1
___ **Breaking and Entering** by Joy Williams	$6.95	394-75773-4
___ **Taking Care** by Joy Williams	$5.95	394-72912-9
___ **The Easter Parade** by Richard Yates	$8.95	679-72230-0
___ **Eleven Kinds of Loneliness** by Richard Yates	$8.95	679-72221-1
___ **Revolutionary Road** by Richard Yates	$8.95	679-72191-6

Now at your bookstore or call toll-free to order: 1-800-638-6460
(credit cards only).